NIGHTWALKER

NIGHTWALKER

NIGHTWALKER™ BOOK ONE

FRANK RODERUS

CRAIG MARTELLE

Nightwalker (this book) is a work of fiction.

All of the characters, organizations, and events portrayed in this novel are either products of the author's imagination or are used fictitiously. Sometimes both.

Nightwalker (and what happens within / characters / situations / worlds) are Copyright (c) 2015 by Frank Roderus (as revised)

Cover by Ryan Schwarz - thecoverdesigner.com
Cover copyright © LMBPN Publishing

Nightwalker is published by LMBPN Publishing

All rights reserved. No part of this publication may be reproduced, stored in a retrieval system, or transmitted in any form or by any means, electronic, mechanical, recording or otherwise, without the prior written permission of LMBPN Publishing. Published under license from the Roderus Estate.

First US edition, April 2019

CHAPTER ONE

I t was time to leave the sanctuary. He had been trying to think back, trying to judge just how long he had been underground. He didn't know. A dozen months? More? Perhaps a good many months. That long since he breathed fresh air, that long since he saw the sun, that long since the war. The war. He thought of it that way, as a war although all he saw were the intense bursts of light and the ugly, pulsing, many colored mushroom clouds grey and yellow and purple, huge cancerous tumors, he shuddered remembering, as an extravagant light display. They might even have been pretty if it were not the end of civilization as he knew it. With that in mind they were not so attractive.

Spokane, Seattle, San Francisco, he was pretty sure those were gone. Certainly there were fireballs in the direction of each. He himself was far enough away, driving an isolated state highway, far enough that he was in no immediate danger. He had time to park the truck, time to climb to the cave opening he remembered seeing on half a dozen runs up this valley in years past, even time enough to open the trailer and drag out several pallets of freeze-dried foods and protein bars. He supposed that was a godsend. He had been hauling a load of Lamb Pins premium quality foods for delivery to an outdoors and health food store in Boise.

Those foods and a trickle of water from the back of the mine kept him alive for all this time. He carried as many cases of the stuff to the tunnel mouth as he could take. They weren't heavy, just bulky. He built a makeshift travois to make the movement quicker to carry more. He unloaded half the trailer before he could carry no more. Along with a few things he had with him in the cab, he then moved everything into the farthest reaches of the mine and stayed there, cold but safe from the airborne radiation that would inevitably have followed the nukes.

He thought he remembered reading that you were supposed to get undercover and stay there if you hoped to avoid radiation. Some accounts had it that you should stay underground for several years. By that time it would be safe to come out again or it never would be.

James Wolfe had no way to tell if it was safe now, if he was underground long enough. What he did know for certain was that he was out of food and could not remain where he was very much longer. He had to come out now whether he wanted to or not.

He stood, picked up the nylon gym bag that held his worldly possessions and began feeling his way along the wall. When he first came into the tunnel it held the big six volt flashlight that he always carried in the toolbox of his rig. He had done his best to conserve the power but the battery died in the first week. Since then—a year, two years or longer, he was not sure—he was in a deep and complete darkness so black that it was literally true he could not see his hand in front of his face. He tried it several times but there was just no light for the eyes to gather.

At first the intense darkness was frightening but that was

a long time ago now. It no longer bothered him. He had adjusted to it. Now darkness seemed normal. Wolfe smiled. Darkness might be normal now but that did not keep him from looking forward to sunlight and moving air. The smell of pine sap, a mountain meadow, salt air coming off the ocean. He remembered those. A pang of anxiety made his chest tighten. What he truly wanted to smell was the salt air coming in off the Gulf of Mexico.

His home if he still had one was far, far away. The job had taken him on the road to Boise but home was Bradenton on the gulf coast of Florida. Home and family. He believed they were still there. Believed they were still alive. He had to believe that or else there would be no point in walking out of this mine and trying to go on. He simply had to believe that.

Wolfe steeled himself and continued making his way along the cold stone walls of the mine as the amount of light showing ahead increased, very bright, very far away. Wolfe hadn't realized just how deep the tunnel ran into the mountain but for all this time he hadn't seen so much as a hint of sunlight nor any other kind of light since the flashlight battery died. It pleased and excited him to see it now and he increased his pace toward the mine entrance. His excitement ended quickly and he stumbled to a halt. The light was too bright, painfully bright, so bright it felt like daggers being driven into his eyes. He blinked, tears rolling down his cheeks, and tried to shield his eyes in the crook of his arm. It did no good. The pain was too intense, the sunlight too strong.

Wolfe leaned against the cold rock and slumped to sit on the floor. He would just have to wait for his eyes to adjust. After all, it had been months, perhaps years since he last saw any sort of light. His eyes must've dilated beyond all reason. He could wait a little longer. Except his eyes did not readjust. The sunlight remained painfully strong.

He rummaged in his gym bag and pulled out a spare shirt and draped that over his head to put a halt to the discomfort. He waited until the sun had set outside before he was able to venture out into the world once again but even so it did not seem dark. There was no moon but the starlight was enough to make everything look as bright as day to him. The only difference was that the shadows were a little deeper, a little darker than he remembered they had been on a sunny day.

The air felt and smelled as magnificent as he hoped to find but apart from that nothing was quite as he expected it to be. The slope of the mountainside was the same as he remembered but where there had been forest now there was only devastation. He was standing in the middle of the world's biggest blowdown; trees tumbled like pick-up sticks, all of them falling toward the southeast.

While he was deep in the tunnel they must have hit Boise too so perhaps this explosion represented a target later on the list. Certainly this one had been closer than the others. He had been fairly far out from Boise when he took refuge in the mine. He tried to remember how far but could not. Still, Boise was virtually due west from the last point of reference he could recall and these trees were felled by a fierce wind from the northwest; however far, the blast and the wind-storm that followed were terrible in its disruptive power. And if the wind was that bad how bad must the radiation have been, perhaps still was.

Wolfe shuddered. Not that there was anything he could do about it. He had to come outside. He had to find a way to go home. He had little expectation that his home still existed, but hoped that his family had made it. They had to even if his home had not.

After all it was only a few miles across open water from MacDill Air Force Base where the US military's Central Command was headquartered. Surely there would've been a few nukes consigned to MacDill, probably several. His hope was that if they, whoever they were—he had no idea who it was who bombed them—if they missed Boise then please God perhaps they missed MacDill too. Perhaps Bradenton, perhaps his home and his loved ones were unharmed.

He made his way carefully through the fallen trees which was made at least a little easier by the fact that all had fallen in one direction. He was able to zigzag down the mountain side to the valley floor and the highway. It was hard for him to see what became of his tractor. The truck had been sent rolling off the hill. It struck hard on the side of the hood and buckled the right front wheel, snapped the axle and crushed the cab.

Wolfe shook his head and managed a small bitter smile. He still owed more than $18,000 on the rugged old Kenworth. He wondered what the finance company intended to do about that now. He walked around to the back of the trailer. He did not know what prompted him to close it before he went up to the mine that last time. The doors were standing open now and there was no sign of the crates of dehydrated foods that had remained there after he exhausted himself carrying much of the load up the hillside. That was all right. Someone had been able to benefit from them. Wolfe could not begrudge them that. He hoped the meals helped them and whoever it was who had come fleeing down this road. He hoped they were able to survive the winds and the radiation.

He made his way past some debris to the front of the rig. He left his sunglasses in the cab when he ran and he was going to need those until his eyes adjusted to the light again.

The driver side of the tractor was not damaged. It rested at an odd angle but there was no reason the door should not open. Probably the sunglasses were still there and the insulated mug that he liked for his coffee. After all this time the thought of coffee hot and steaming was enough to make his mouth water. More than chicken fried steak or a juicy hamburger right now it was coffee that made his empty stomach rumble.

Wolfe approached the step and reached for the grab bar then drew back, his brows knitting in puzzled concern. He could feel a sort of tingling sensation coming off the metal, almost like the steel was humming but very faintly. He reached for the bar again but stopped short of touching it. There was something not right about the feeling he was getting. It felt dangerous, somehow wrong as if his flesh was giving him a warning. He took a step back toward the trailer and reached out as if to place his palm on the frame. Again his hand tingled except it was not exactly a tingle that he felt, more like a buzzing noise that he could not hear. Hearing was not the right word for it. It was a sensation he never had before, much like he was hearing something through his skin not his ears. The feeling was strange and he did not like it. He pulled his hand back. Radiation perhaps, he thought. You could not see, hear or taste radiation, but that seemed the logical conclusion. Radiation affected metal more than anything else and his rig had been sitting out here exposed to the effects of the Boise explosion and perhaps that of other bombs as well. It could well have been exposed enough that it was radioactive now.

Wolfe shuddered. Contact with contaminated metal could kill you. He was certain he had heard that or read it somewhere. Funny but he no longer had any interest in climbing up into the cabin to retrieve his sunglasses or the mug. He turned away wondering what had become of other people who looted his cargo in the aftermath of the bombs. Come to think of it, he wondered what had become of everyone who passed this way while he was safe inside the mine tunnel. Had the truck's supplies saved their lives, or only prolonged their misery? A frightening thought occurred to him. Surely he could not be the last living human. He shuddered again. That of course would be too much. He would find others and he would find his way back home to Lurleen and Jojo laughing, shrieking and running through the house.

Wolfe wiped impatiently at his eyes. He must have gotten some dust in them. He stood and took a long breath. Home was that way. He started walking.

CHAPTER TWO

He slowed then came to a complete stop, head lifted, nostrils flaring. It took a moment to identify the scent. There was smoke somewhere not far ahead. There was fire and fire almost surely meant the presence of people for he had seen no indication of recent storms. Wolfe was anxious to see people again, to talk, to find out just what it was that happened. He did not even know who the enemy was or who had won the nuclear war.

Wolfe cleared his throat. It had been all those months, however many he still did not know since he had not spoken to anyone. For a moment he was afraid he would not be able to speak. Experimentally and feeling self-conscious about it he muttered a few soft hellos into the night. His throat was raw and his voice gravelly but at least he could form the words and get them out. His fears were silly. He knew that but felt them anyway. He wondered what he would look like, coming at them out of the night like this. He was what his grandfather used to call middling tall, about 5 foot 11 and lean enough after all this time on short rations. But then he had always been in good shape. It was nothing he worked at, just genetics he supposed.

He had dark hair, long now after all this time without being cut. He wore jeans, a plaid shirt and hiking boots, comfortable things he had worn when he was pushing his rig. They were rumpled but he had tried to keep them clean, scrubbing them as best he could in the little stream that collected at the back of the mine and ran through to the outside. He hoped he could put up a presentable appearance for these people whoever they were.

Wolfe's pace quickened and then he hurried down the cluttered highway, dodging tree trunks and the occasional abandoned vehicle toward the source of smoke there on his left and partway up a hillside.

He could see a faint glow of dying coals. He had been walking for several hours and hadn't started until well after nightfall so by now it was sometime in the middle of the night. He hoped the people who built the fire were still there. Hoped, too, that they would not mind being awakened by a stranger at this hour. That was a chance he had to take although he should be conscious about how he approached these people. He thought he should look the camp over before he walked in and announced himself. Just in case.

Wolfe hiked up the hillside, avoiding the tangle of fallen trees and loose rock. It still amazed him that he could see so clearly. Even now with no moon at all he could see as easily as if it were day.

The glowing fire ring was situated beside a small spring that seeped out of the hillside thirty feet or so short of the camp. Wolfe stood behind some slender saplings while he looked the camp over.

Two people were stretched out on the ground wrapped snug in sleeping bags. A third, a woman, sat leaning up against the trunk of what must've been a fairly good-sized tree, although now all that was left of it was a 6-inch-thick stub that extended for five feet off the ground. Everything above that was gone. Wolfe could not imagine the destructive power that swept through here but seeing that effect this far away from the center of the blast made him ache for those who would have been caught by it. Yet there were some who had survived. He himself was proof enough of that and now these three.

He was about to speak when the woman beside the tree trunk shifted. She moved her shoulders and tried to find a more comfortable position. It was only then that he saw she was not leaning against the tree by choice; she was tied in place there, her arms drawn behind her and her wrists secured on the other side of the trunk.

There was pain in her expression and cold, sorrowful hopelessness. Wolfe frowned. He supposed there might be a perfectly good reason why the two who were sleeping held the woman captive but instead of speaking out and waking the two he slipped silently forward.

The woman was staring in his direction but did not seem to see him. That puzzled him for a moment until he remembered that it was dark. He could see perfectly well but she could not.

Wolfe moved stealthily forward until he was standing beside the nearer of the pair of sleepers. It was a man wearing a full, very dark beard. A shotgun lay on the ground beside him. Wolfe reached for the gun, not wanting it but not wanting the man to come awake shooting either. He intended only to set it aside where the man could not reach it when he woke up. Wolfe stopped short of touching the weapon though he felt the same buzzy tingle coming off the shotgun that he first felt back at his rig. He was reasonably certain the tingle was caused by radiation. The gun was dangerously hot.

He could not understand why in the world this man would choose to carry the gun when it could sicken and even kill him. Wolfe quickly redirected his motion and took hold of the shotgun by the wooden stock to pick it up and very quickly got rid of it, pitching it down the far side of a couple of juniper. Even though he knew it was irrational he felt like washing his hands after touching the contaminated gun. Only the metal parts would actually be dangerous but still Wolfe stepped around the bearded man and approached the other, He heard a gasp of alarm from the woman. She must have seen him now but she said nothing,

He found a weapon beside the other man, a compound bow all cables and spidery bits that work much better than the old wooden longbow Wolfe had as a boy. This one had a quiver, very wicked looking arrows attached to the right side and a leather keeper sort of thing that he did not fully understand. At least the ball was not contaminated by radiation, everything considered. Wolfe decided to hang on to the weapon until he worked out who was in the right. He did not want any misunderstandings of the sort that could lead to violence. He picked up the bow and carried it well away from the fire and the sleeping men. Only then did he return to the camp and approach the woman. He knelt beside her and whispered, "Who are you and why are you tied up like this?"

"Oh God, don't hurt me, please don't hurt me."

"I'm not going to hurt you, miss. Why are you tied up? Did you do something wrong? Are these men police or something?"

She looked at him like he was crazy. "Mister. There's no police in the red zone. These guys are wilders. I was living in the clear area but close to the line. They kidnapped me and took me along to serve them…you know what I mean…and cook and things like that. Kidnapped, it's more common than you might think. I mean the thing about scavenging, it isn't the sort of thing a woman is likely to do. So if a guy wants to go wilding he's going have to find a woman in the clear area and take her with him. If he wants one along that is. I guess there's some that don't bother."

Wolfe frowned. He had no idea what this woman meant by all the zones and areas and such. Wilding. Scavenging. He did not know what those were and this did not seem like the time to ask. He could do that later.

"Lady, I am going to cut you free. If you want to get away from these guys you can go wherever you like."

"Yes, yes please."

His lock blade pocket knife took quick care of the ropes that bound the woman's wrists. He helped her get to her feet.

"Just a minute. My legs are going to sleep. Let me stretch for a bit, okay?" She spoke in a normal voice, forgetting to whisper.

"Rub your wrists and move your arms and legs around." Wolfe closed the knife and dropped it back into his pocket whispering, "I think we better go now before those two wake up."

The admonition was too late. One of the men was awake. And he was angry. He came out of his sleeping bag in a rush and, roaring, charged straight at Wolfe with murder in his eyes and a foot-long knife in his fist.

CHAPTER THREE

Wolfe should have been scared half to death, probably would have been if he had time for fear. Jim Wolfe was no brawler. He had not had a fistfight since he was in the eighth grade. And he lost that fight.

The man with the knife was half a head taller than Wolfe and sixty pounds heavier, not all of which was lard. Wolfe dropped into a crouch and held himself motionless watching the big man's charge. His blood surged through his veins like molten steel and he felt the slabs of muscle across his shoulders swell. There was a prickling sensation across the back of his neck.

The man was roaring. Wolfe responded with a low growling howl that ripped from his throat without conscious thought. Reacting without taking time to think about what he was going to do, he stepped into the charge and slashed the back of his left hand across the wrist of the hand that held the knife. He heard the muted crack of brittle bone being shattered and the bearded man screamed in pain, the knife clattering to the ground.

Wolfe met the force of the charge by striking the big

man's forehead with his right hand. The blow snapped the man's head back and sent him upright. Wolfe grabbed the man's belt with his left hand and the unprotected leg with his right. He used what was left of the fellow's momentum to lift him overhead, spinning him around. With a snarl Wolfe spun, driving with legs and arms alike. The big man cried out in terror as he was lofted into the air, arms and legs flailing. He fell to earth with an ugly thud a good thirty feet distant.

By then the second man was out of his sleeping bag and rushing to join his companion's attack. He brandished a revolver and was shouting something but when he saw what Wolfe had done to the first man, the huge body flung aside as if it were a department store mannequin, he blinked in disbelief and stumbled to a halt, shock and confusion registering on his face. Wolfe slapped the revolver aside then grabbed the man's throat, sweeping him around. He had not meant to but he heard the neck snap half a second before that one went flying into the air.

Wolfe stood motionless in the cool night air, his muscles bulging and a red haze of fury clouding his vision. He dipped his head back and yelled his victory to the stars.

CHAPTER FOUR

"How did you do that?" the woman whispered, her lowered voice this time due to awe and not caution. "I never saw anything like that before, the way you just…just threw them like that.

"I don't know," Wolfe told her honestly. "I just did it."

"You're awfully strong for an old guy."

An old guy? He was thirty-two years old. She looked to be a good ten years older than he, a nice enough looking woman but certainly older than he was.

"Are you going to hurt me?" she asked. "Are you going to…you know…keep me for a slave?"

"Lord no, ma'am. You can do whatever you want. I'd like to talk to you for a minute, though. There are a lot of things I want to ask you about, but you can do whatever you like. I don't want to hurt you any. And those men aren't going to hurt you either. I can promise you that."

He felt pretty confident about that claim. One of them was dead. Wolfe was sure of that, for he heard that one's neck snap. The other one had a broken arm and maybe worse, which reminded him. He walked over to where the first one, the big fellow, had landed. That man was still alive anyway. He was not fully conscious but he was breathing and moving around a little bit.

Wolfe left the man lying where he was and returned to the remains of the fire where the woman was busy building the flame again. "Is there anything to eat here?" Wolfe asked.

"Yes, of course. Would you like me to fix something for you?"

"If you wouldn't mind."

She went to a small cart loaded with nylon duffels. The cart looked like one of those aluminum carts designed to be pulled behind bicycles. She began digging into the things there. While she was doing that, Wolfe found the weapons the men had had, the shotgun and the wicked-looking, but rather confusing, bow. The shotgun was dangerously radioactive judging by the tingle coming from its metal whenever his hand came near. Wolf picked the gun up by the wooden butt stock and smashed it against the rocks until it was broken and thoroughly useless.

The bow was lying on the ground. Wolfe felt it very carefully before he picked it up. There was no tingle of radioactivity this time so he went back to the injured man and unfastened the fellow's belt then removed the sheath for the fighting knife. He threaded that onto his own belt.

"That's my knife," the man protested weakly.

"It used to be. Now it's mine," Wolfe said.

The man lay quiet for several moments. Then he nodded.

"Thank you." Wolfe held his hand close to the blued steel of the second man's revolver. It was as hot as the shotgun had been. Wolfe picked it up by poking a stick through the trigger guard and sent it flying far down the hillside. It hit with a clatter but Wolfe did not know if it was damaged. Hopefully it would stay lost.

"Tell me something," he said to the man who was

conscious now even if unhappy and in pain. "Did you want to risk dying for those guns? Are you mad? Why would you walk around carrying something that's hot? Can't you feel it when you touch them?"

"Mister, you can't feel radioactivity. You can't taste or smell or feel it and the guys we got those off said they were all right."

"Then they lied to you. Both of them are hot. You really couldn't feel the radiation?"

"You mean you really could?"

"Sure. It feels kind of...I don't know. Buzzing. Like the metal is vibrating real, real fast.

"You're crazy."

Wolfe shrugged. "That may be but if I was you I'd get myself looked at for the burns or whatever that stuff did to you.

The man went pale. "I'll, uh, maybe find a doc out in the clear areas. What do you think?"

Wolfe had a look at his good arm, his hand and forearm. They showed a telltale rash on them. Wolfe could see there was a rash on the broken arm as well.

The man began to cry. "Are there doctors in the, what's it called, clear area? Are there doctors there who know what to do with radiation poisoning?"

"There isn't much I can do."

"You have to help me, mister." It was the big man who was whispering now.

Wolfe shrugged. This man tried to kill him tonight. He supposed he should feel compassion. The fellow did not know it but he was already dying. Wolfe could not find a way to care about the man. If he wanted to die because of his own greed and stupidity he was welcome to do so. He said, "Get out. Stand up and walk away from here. I don't want you around where I camp."

"You can't make me do that, mister. I'm hurt bad."

"I can, and I am," Wolfe said. "Now get out. Take yourself back to where you came from. And if I was you I'd see a doctor about what those guns did to you. Now do whatever you please but right now you're walking away from this camp or else you won't have to worry about doctors or walking anyplace ever again." Wolfe was not sure he meant that but he did not trust this man and did not want him anywhere around. "Now go. Right now."

"You can't…"

Wolfe took hold of the fellow's shirt front and picked the man up as easily as if he were a sack of onions. A small sack. The man's eyes went wide at the effortless way Wolfe plucked him off the ground, and he became pale again. Not only was he tall, he was thick through the torso and legs as well and heavily muscled. He probably weighed well over 250 pounds. Wolfe was amazed himself that it took no effort at all to pick him up.

"Let me go get my stuff."

"No," Wolfe snarled. "You'll go now or not at all."

The big man went, head down, scurrying down the hillside to the highway.

"Breakfast is ready," the woman said.

Wolfe had to shield his eyes from the bright flames. It hurt to look anywhere near them but the smell of frying meat reminded him of how long it had been since he had eaten anything at all and how much longer since he had anything substantial.

CHAPTER FIVE

Wolfe pulled a piece of gristle out of his mouth and tossed it onto the coals. Now that the fire was dying again he could stand to glance at it although he could not bear to look directly at the ash coated red coals. The cartilage snapped and popped.

"Miss, can I ask you something?" Wolfe said.

"Sure, anything."

"This will probably sound stupid but how long has it been since the war?"

She gave him a questioning look but did answer. "Just over two, maybe two and a half years."

"That long." He shook his head. "I lost track. I hope you won't mind if I keep asking some things."

"Mister, I owe you pretty much everything so anything you want answered, just ask. A few questions are nothing. Not after you got me away from those wilders."

"Now that's something right there," he said. "Wilders. You called them that before. So what does that mean exactly?"

She frowned and thought for a moment. "I suppose you'd say it's one of those things that you know when you see it even if you can't exactly put a box around it or draw pictures. You can mean sometimes one thing, sometimes another, depending. You really don't know any of this stuff? It's like you been off somewhere ever since it happened."

Wolfe nodded. "I was inside a mine, haven't seen the light of day nor spoke with another human being from that day forward. Now I don't know a thing that's happened since."

"I see. Let me set you straight as much as I can. Wilders, that's somebody that comes over here into the red zone to scavenge for whatever useful stuff they can find and then smuggle it back over the border into the clear area. That accounts for some of them that you would call wilders. And then there's others or so they say that just go wild because they don't want to obey nobody's laws. They don't want anybody telling them what to do so they leave the clear area. Here it's all right for them to do whatever they like. By the way, you can pass out of the clear if you want to. The border still does have some rules. Not many but that's one of them. You can leave the clear, you just can't get back in so easy from the red zone. See, if you do it legal you got to be in quarantine to make sure you aren't diseased, and everything you have with you that's metal or any food or most any possession at all is impounded by the Federal Command."

She sat back on her heels. "I guess you wouldn't know about that either. What government there is, is run by the Federal Command." She turned her head and spat, as if spitting on the title itself. "Everything is under control of those bastards. There is no more state or local government authority, none. It's calm now but FEDCOM troopers, they got the right to do pretty much anything they want. They can even shoot a citizen if they want. That is supposed to be only for cause but the troopers are human. They can be as ugly as anybody. Lots of them are bullies. If you make one of them mad he can pop you. There's nothing to be done about it either. I know. My oldest boy Tommy, him and two friends, they was caught trying to steal some food to stretch our rations.

"Tommy was lucky. He got shot through both legs but he'll be all right again. One of his buddies was killed."

"You say rations. What is that about?" he asked.

"Almost everything is rationed. What little bit is available. Food especially is in short supply but at least there is some, enough to keep a body going. There is no tobacco or razor blades or alcohol, no ammunition at all. Not that that makes so much difference because there's not supposed to be any private ownership of guns. Of course most everybody we know has something hidden away. The most valuable stuff, what the scavengers want the most to smuggle back into the clear areas are cigarettes and whiskey. I guess most places are pretty well picked over already so they have to go farther and farther in order to find anything worth hauling back with them."

Wolfe picked up a pebble and turned it over in his fingers. It sounded like the whole world had turned upside down since the war. "Could I ask you something else?"

"Of course."

"Who was it that did this to us?"

"You don't even know that?"

He shook his head.

"North Korea started it then once it got going good, China and India jumped in too."

"So who won?"

"It isn't over yet. They still fight. FEDCOM doesn't allow much real news to get out but we understand our ground troops are in Russia now trying to keep the Chinese from getting their hands on the old Soviet nukes. I guess they've already used up everything they had. The Chinese, I mean. So now we're fighting them on the ground in Russia to keep the Chinese out of there and drop our nukes on them. Thank goodness we had enough on hand when it began. I guess we dropped a lot on China and just about wiped out North Korea but we don't have a lot of allies which Russia is being one. We mostly stand alone. Or so they tell us.

"It sounds like a mess," Wolfe said.

"Yes it does and it is. Say, can I ask you something now?"

"Go ahead."

The woman smiled. "What's your name? Mine is Reba, Reba Crane."

He introduced himself adding, "Wolfe with an e on it."

"You're kind of Native American aren't you, Mr. Wolfe?"

He shook his head. "No, I'm not even a little bit native."

She said, "I may be just the tiniest bit myself. I was told once that we have a speck of Delaware in the family but that was so far back it wouldn't count. The reason I bring it up, I mean, you not having any beard or anything. Most all menfolk have beards now except the rich and some of that, officers and like that."

"I never paid any attention," Wolfe said. "After all this time I should have a beard but I just never thought about it." Wolfe ran a hand over his chin. His face was as smooth as a young boy's.

"There's another thing," the woman said. "When I first saw you I took you to be an old guy. No offense but up close you're a young guy."

"Why would you have thought that?"

She laughed. "If I was you I'd look at yourself in the mirror. But now that you're sitting still and close up I can see that you got shoulders on you like that Arnold what's his name."

"Schwarzenegger?"

"That's him."

"When I was in the mine I couldn't see to do anything

useful so I'd spent most of my time doing isometric exercises."

"I suppose that would account for it," Reba said.

"What's wrong with my hair other than being so long?" Wolfe asked.

She gave him an odd look. "Nothing is wrong with it exactly, just that your hair is white as fresh snow. It looks long enough you can pull it around and see for yourself."

She was not playing a trick on him. His hair had no color at all. White hair, no beard, that thing about being able to feel radiation coming off objects when you really were not supposed to be able to. And of course all that strength that he had not really expected, certainly had not had before he went into the mine. Wolfe wondered what else might have happened to him while he was in that tunnel and what caused it; some sort of filtered radiation exposure or maybe there had been some kind of isotopes or whatever in the water that trickled into the mine.

He felt fine. If anything he felt stronger and more fit now than he had ever been in his life. But if there turned out to be something badly wrong with him, radiation poisoning or such, well, he hoped he would live long enough to get home to Lurleen and Jojo.

"Is there anything wrong?" Reba said. "You're frowning."

Wolfe shook his head. "No, nothing." His attention though was elsewhere, far away on the Gulf Coast of Florida. *Lord*, he thought, *let them still live. Let them know that I still love them.*

CHAPTER SIX

Daybreak was agony for him. The first shaft of sunlight to come streaming over the hills felt like spear points being driven straight into his eyes. Even closing his eyes was not enough to protect them from the agony. Wolfe fumbled another one of the sleeping bags the scavengers had been using and draped it over his head. Tears were running down his face and he was shaking from the pain.

"What's wrong?" Reba asked.

Wolfe shook his head. "The sunlight. It hurts something awful and I don't know why. I never used to be so sensitive to light. Now I can't stand it. I can see in the dark just fine but I can't abide bright daylight."

"I wish I had some sunglasses for you. You need something to cut the light. It wouldn't be good if a gang of wilders caught you in daytime. You can't defend yourself if you can't see."

"Would they do something to a passing stranger?"

"Mr. Wolfe, some of those men would kill you just for the chance to examine your pockets. Even if you didn't have anything worth taking. There are some, or so I'm told, would kill you so they can bet on which way the blood would run. You don't want to be anyplace in the red zone without being able to defend yourself."

"Well there's nothing I can do about it now. Not until dark. There's no way I could see anything before then."

Reba shuddered. "What if Harvey comes back?"

"Who's Harvey?"

"That's the scavenger with the broken arm. You killed his partner and took his stuff. Who knows but what he could find some other wilders and tell them you have a haul of whiskey in that cart or something just to get back at you for messing them up like you did."

"You have a wicked mind, Mrs. Crane."

"I come by it honest enough from bitter experience. Believe me I was happy just being an ordinary housewife in Big Piney."

"Big Piney," Wolfe repeated. "I've seen that on the map. It's over in Wyoming, isn't it?"

She nodded and inclined her head to the left. "It's across the line there. It isn't far."

"Your husband, is he all right?

"He's fine. At least I expect he is. He and my boys were all working when those wilders came. That's one thing right now. A body can always find work building fence for the FEDCOM. They want to fence off the whole border between all the clear areas and the dead zones. Never mind that it will take years to do and cost who knows how much, money that could be better used for something else and never mind neither that a fence never kept the immigrants out along the southern border. They are bound and determined to do it anyhow. But at least it gives us work and puts some food on the table."

"What I was saying though is that they was off working when Harvey and Brinks, he's the dead one lying over there on the rocks, they came by and found me alone. Wanted me for, well you know what men will do to a woman. So they walked in and took me and headed west into the red zone. They've kept me tied up ever since. I would've picked up a big rock and smashed their skulls open. I'm glad you did it for Brinks, and I wish you'd done the same for Harvey. If he shows himself again, be my guest. I'll hold him down for you."

Wolfe said, "That isn't something to kid about.

"I am not kidding. I would do it in a heartbeat."

"I guess I would too," Wolfe said and was more than a little surprised to discover that he was telling the truth. It was a funny thing to discover that the veneer of civilization was thinner than he would have thought. It seemed that the world around them had reverted to savagery, and he would have to become just as savage if he wanted to get back to Lurleen and JoJo. But because of them he had survived and would continue surviving, no matter what.

"I just thought of something," Reba said after a moment. "Can you wait here for a minute?"

"Believe me, I'm not going anywhere with my eyes hurting this bad." Wolfe sat huddled underneath the sleeping bag, eyes tightly closed. He listened as Mrs. Crane went hurrying away in the direction of the baggage cart.

CHAPTER SEVEN

"I feel really, really silly," Wolfe declared.

"Yes but can you see?" she asked.

He blinked, rubbed his eyes then very cautiously peeled the heavy sleeping bag off the top of his head. The sunlight was still bright but he could see.

"Everything looks a little fuzzy," he told her.

"Of course it does. You're looking through two layers of nylon pantyhose. It ought to be fuzzy."

Wolfe grinned. "It works. It's crazy but it works. Thank you."

"Thank you? A lousy thank you is all I get for my almost last pair of pantyhose?" Reba laughed.

"I could…I don't know how much money I have in my wallet but it should be a couple hundred dollars or so."

"Hold on there, mister. I was joking with you. Besides, dollars aren't worth anything anymore. They took those out of circulation right away. It's one of the ways the FEDCOM uses to exert control. All that old-style money went back to being just pieces of paper although practically everybody hoards them, hoping someday things will go back to being the way they used to be. Personally I wouldn't count on it."

Wolfe smiled and looked around. It was broad daylight but he could see, not well but he could make out shapes well enough. "The colors seem to be a little off when seen through…did you say two layers of this stuff?"

"Uh-huh. I cut the top strip off. That's the thick part that's supposed to flatten your tummy or in your case squeeze your head. I folded that piece over. I figured one layer wouldn't do all that much. Like a bank robber, they can see through stockings just fine and their eyesight is normal, so I figured with yours so sensitive, well, you should have two layers. Besides you're twice as good as a bank robber." She laughed.

"This is a solution I never would have thought of, but it seems to work. Thank you, Reba. Thinking about banks, I guess there aren't any now. No banks, no insurance companies either. And I would guess all debt was wiped out by those bombs." Wolfe smiled. "Like they say, a silver lining for every cloud no matter how stormy."

Reba giggled then said, "My pantyhose look good enough on you but really, with your coloring your proper shade should be suntan."

Wolfe roared with laughter. Mrs. Crane was feeling good. That was all right. So was he, and he could see in the daylight now, at least a little, with her makeshift light filter pulled over his eyes. Bands of material she took from the upper leg of a pair of pantyhose no doubt was more like a headband. It tended to drift too far south, and the rig undoubtedly looked every bit as silly as he felt. But that didn't matter at all. It worked. That was the important thing. He could defend them if wilders showed up and tried to stir up trouble.

"Mrs. Crane, let's pack up this outfit and get on the road."

"Where to?"

He thought she sounded a little nervous when she asked

that. He said, "The first thing will be to get you back to Big Piney and your family. After that I like to think that I still have a family to go home to as well."

Reba looked considerably relieved. Fuzzy or not, he could see well enough to tell that much. "Thank you. It isn't terribly far. Those two weren't exactly what you would call diligent in the pursuit of their trade. You know they wanted a bottle along the way and…and to do things."

"I'm sorry about that, Mrs. Crane, but it's good they hadn't taken you so awfully far. Now if you'd give me some idea about where we're going, we can get on with it."

"Five minutes. Give me five minutes and we'll be on our way."

CHAPTER EIGHT

"Slow down."

"Sorry," he told her. Reba was a trooper and tried her best to keep up but sometimes Wolfe forgot.

"Can we take a break?"

"Sure." He left the cart sitting in the middle of the road. It wasn't like anyone was going to come along and run into it. Unfortunately. He had not seen any sort of moving vehicles, not on the ground nor for that matter in the air either.

He led the way to a slab of stone beneath the shade of huge pine. They had been walking for the better part of two days and were nearly clear of the vast swathes of trees that had been blown down by the hot winds generated by the nuclear bombs. Wolfe was not sure if they were outdistancing the effects of the wind or if the hills that lay between here and the nearest Ground Zero had given protection to the trees. Whatever the reason, it was nice to be traveling on clear roads again. Further north it had been like walking through some fantasy giant's pile of pickup sticks. They still passed the occasional car or truck that was either abandoned or wrecked. Some of the wrecked vehicles held the decaying, skeletal remains of their owners. All of them whether wrecked or abandoned had long since been ransacked for anything of value, and so far every one of them gave off that buzzing tingle of radiation that Wolfe had come to accept even though he could not understand it.

"How're we doing?" he asked as he helped himself to a seat on the rock.

Reba smiled. "We're getting there."

Wolfe produced a handkerchief and wiped his face.

"We need to talk," she said.

"All right."

"We're out of fresh meat. We still have plenty of rice and beans and some dry stuff. And a couple cans of this and that." She made a face and Wolfe guessed she was still angry that he made her get rid of most of the canned goods that the scavengers had been carrying. Some of the cans had been bloated, others badly dented. Wolfe had not wanted to take a chance that they might be contaminated, but he had had difficulty trying to convince Reba about his concerns. He doubted that she believed him even now, but she had allowed him to pitch the suspect food. That was the important thing.

"We should give some thought to finding fresh meat," she said.

Wolfe blinked, the folded pantyhose covering his eyes catching at his eyelashes rather uncomfortably when he did so. He had not really considered what he would have to do about food in the future. Reba would be going home to her family so he would have to feed only himself, but it was a long, long way home. Besides, the food in the cart properly belonged to her.

He was no outdoorsman who knew what wild foods were safe to eat for him to live off the land. He had no idea which plants were food at all never mind the other kind. Nor was he much of a hunter. The only hunting he had done in his whole life, if you could call it that, was when he was ten or eleven and had a BB gun. Then he had been the scourge of the neighborhood. No songbird was safe from him.

Actually he would have been happy to have that BB gun back now. Song bird soup was sure to be nourishing. As it was, well, they did see deer now and then, and this morning they had gotten a glimpse of a moose or an elk off in the distance. There were rabbits and squirrels and small birds and surely there must be domesticated cattle roaming loose, whatever of them the scavengers had not already found and driven back to the clear area.

The obvious but not necessarily simple answer was to use the compound bow to hunt the wild game…if only he knew how to use the darn thing. He never in his life hunted with a bow and was much more comfortable with the folding pocketknife or his new belt knife but neither of them was going to be much help as a hunting weapon.

The matter of acquiring food was something he was really going to have to give some thought to, he realized. "Are we all right for now?" he asked.

"We're fine except meat. We still have some of that but it's starting to spoil. I don't think it will last much longer."

"Is it still good for tonight?"

"Yes, I think so."

Wolfe smiled. "Then let's have ourselves a feast tonight, Mrs. Crane. Pick out whatever looks to be still good and let's cook all of it. We'll gorge ourselves to celebrate."

"Celebrate what, Mr. Wolfe?"

"Why, we can celebrate being alive, Mrs. Crane. Can you think of any better reason?"

"Come to think of it, no, I guess I can't."

"Then I'll tell you what," Wolfe said. "It's fairly late in the afternoon and we're not on what you would call a tight schedule. You drag out the meat and decide what is good while I get some wood and get a fire started. We'll make camp right here and settle down for an evening of good food and excellent company. We can get a good night's sleep and be raring to go again in the morning."

"Say no more, Mr. Wolfe. I accept your invitation. She went to fetch the cart off the highway and Wolfe began gathering fallen wood, enough to maintain a good fire for hours and have some left over for morning. Being alive really was reason enough for a celebration, he thought, whistling softly as he worked.

CHAPTER NINE

olfe took an inventory of sorts, frowning most of
the time. Much of what he found was useless. There
were two shoeboxes, for instance, filled with very carefully
arranged currency, most of it hundreds but with some fifties
and twenties as well. He had no way to judge how much was
there, thousands probably, but he had no intention of
wasting his time counting it. Money was useless now, Mrs.
Crane said.

He gathered that the wilders who forced Mrs. Crane out
of her home were among those who could not believe the
paper no longer had value. They must have been collecting it
everywhere they went and glorying in their paper wealth.
But then these men were criminals and no one ever said
criminals were smart. Ask any cop about that.

There were also two boxes of 38 special cartridges and a
box and a half of 12 gauge number two shotgun shells. They
had three sleeping bags and some spare clothing but no soap
or scissors, one half filled butane cigarette lighter but no
matches, a small box holding a handful of gaudy jewelry that

might have been real but might as easily have been dime store stuff. All Wolfe was really interested in was the bow and the arrows. There were six arrows fitted in the hard rubber quiver that was bolted on the side of the bow and another eight wrapped in a piece of oilcloth carried in the cart, all of them with fiberglass shafts with very nasty looking three bladed hunting-type broadheads.

Wolfe had not shot any sort of bow since he was a kid, and then it had been nothing remotely like this space-age contraption with that system of pulleys and pegs. He did remember, though, that arrows are not indestructible. They can be reused indefinitely right up until the time they break or become lost. One thing he remembered for sure was that a brightly colored target arrow could be lost forever beneath the surface of a backyard lawn even if it traveled no more than ten yards and the archer saw exactly where the arrow stuck.

Wolfe smiled a little recalling his father fussing at him for losing half his arrows the first day he had the bow. The old man grumbled and moaned bitterly about it but that same evening he drove Jimmy over to the hobby shop and bought another dozen arrows for twenty-five cents apiece.

Lord, that it been a long time ago now. More than twenty years but the now-grown Jim Wolfe with a boy of his own could remember it clearly. He wished he someday soon would be able to teach his own son how to shoot a bow and fish for food and everything.

Wolfe shook himself out of his reverie and began looking for an embankment of soft earth where he could get in some practice and hopefully avoid losing his arrows. The sensible thing, he supposed, would be to choose just one arrow to practice with. The razor sharp blades were bound to be damaged by the dirt and small stones, and he did not want all of his few arrows damaged.

He left Mrs. Crane to tend their supper while he took the bow and walked down the road looking for a suitable place to shoot.

CHAPTER TEN

Thanks to his pantyhose headband Wolfe could enjoy the fire not just the warmth and the fresh pine scent of it but the sight of it too and he especially enjoyed the aroma of roasting meat. He reached for another piece.

"Mrs. Crane, you're a fine cook." He grinned. "Everything considered."

"Everything considered indeed but to tell you the truth," Reba said, "I'd still rather have a whopper." She sighed. "The nearest Burger King used to be down in Kemmerer. We wouldn't get down there but maybe once every month or two. Every time, though, we loaded up on whoppers. I expect I won't see one of those again, not in this lifetime."

"You never know. Maybe some smart businessman will bring fast food back." Wolfe frowned and peered off down the road then glanced toward the sky. It was late afternoon but there was still good daylight left, too much perhaps. It would be an hour at least before his vision became normal after the fading of the sunlight.

"What is it, Mr. Wolfe?"

"We're about to have company and I'm not sure I like the looks of them, but let's be fair. Let's wait and see. They may be innocent travelers."

"Whatever you say, Mr. Wolfe," Reba said. She sounded nervous when she said it, though.

There were three men. And they were not innocent. When they came to Wolfe and Reba the three grinned evilly, almost licking their chops to find a good looking woman and what appeared to be a blind old man. And with a cart full of treasure too.

"Do what we say and you might be all right," a bearded man wearing a sweatshirt growled.

"Give up your stuff if you don't want trouble," a second man wearing a baseball cap warned.

The third, a lean man wearing a long billed cap with an assortment of fisherman's flies stuck in the crown, held back, saying nothing but appearing to Wolfe to be a little troubled by the thought of stealing.

"Don't hurt us," Wolfe said.

"Give us any trouble and we'll hurt the hell out o' you. Now give it up," sweatshirt said.

"No trouble," Wolfe said. He shuffled his feet and groped with his hands to keep up the pretense that he was blind. He wanted to get close before they realized their mistake. There were, after all, three of them.

"I said you should sit down old man. Right now before you make me mad," ball cap said. Behind him sweatshirt chuckled and tried to slip silently around the side for what he intended to be a sneak attack on a man he thought was both blind and elderly like Mrs. Crane thought at first. These men believed him to be old because of the snowy white hair he had since he came out of the mine tunnel. That was their second mistake. And their last.

Wolfe acted as if he did not know sweatshirt was there

and headed slowly toward the men. The fisherman looked uncomfortable but did nothing to try to stop his friends.

"Are you going to sit down and be quiet or are we going to have to hurt you?" ball cap asked.

"You just might have to hurt me then," Wolfe said.

Ball cap nodded to his buddy sweatshirt who was now standing at Wolfe's side. Sweatshirt rolled his eyes and motioned a "watch this" gesture to ball cap. Smiling, he wound up to throw a punch at Wolfe's unprotected face. Or what he believed to be a blind man's unprotected head.

Wolfe waited until sweatshirt's punch was thrown then caught it in the palm of his left hand, reaching for it like snatching a fly out of the air.

Sweatshirt cried out "hey," startled but not concerned. Until Wolfe squeezed. Hard.

Wolfe heard the crackle of breaking bones and sweatshirt screamed in pain. With his left hand Wolfe whipped sweatshirt's arm downward while at the same time driving his right hand upward into the underside of sweatshirt's elbow. That joint broke as well and sweatshirt passed out cold from the pain.

Wolfe let sweatshirt fall to the ground then leaped forward, taking ball cap by the throat and the crotch. He held the man aloft for a moment then slammed him down on the ground. Ball cap hit the ground hard. Wolfe heard something break and ball cap writhed back and forth in sudden agony for a moment then lay still.

"No," the fishermen whispered. "Please no, mister, please."

Wolfe was already poised to strike the man down. He did not have any conscious memory of approaching the fisherman, but he was there in front of the man. He had done it so quickly and in such a rage that he simply had no recollection of the act.

"Oh, God, please, mister, please." He cried, drawing back from Wolfe's fury. "Please."

Wolfe took a long, deep breath. He was trembling. Blood still pounded hot in his veins and there was a red haze over his vision. It took him a moment to regain control of himself enough that he could speak.

"Get your friends. Go away. Do it now."

"Yes sir, yes sir, thank you sir." The fisherman bobbed his head and bowed low, obviously still terrified of Wolfe.

"Leave those guns you have in your belts," Wolfe ordered.

"Yes, sir. I'm sorry, sir."

"Don't be all day."

"Whatever you say, sir," he said, bending low and struggling to lift ball cap, at the same time bobbing his head vigorously up and down. Fisherman took his own pistol and laid it gently on the ground, plucked a revolver out of ball cap's belt and put it aside as well. Sweatshirt quickly complied too, taking out an automatic of some kind and laying it down.

"Can I use the cart? This man is dead weight." the fisherman asked.

"I don't care what you two do with him later but get all three of you out of our campsite."

The fisherman knelt beside sweatshirt and prodded at him until sweatshirt got up off the ground, cradling his broken arm. The fisherman opened a small knife, looking cautiously to be sure Wolfe did not take offense, and cut an opening in the front of sweatshirt's shirt, very gently pushed his hand inside so the shirt itself would support the man's broken arm and act like a sling.

Sweatshirt was pale and slick with cold sweat by the time fisherman was done. Between them they got ball cap loaded onto a grocery cart. It was almost fully dark by the time they were done and Wolfe pulled the pantyhose light filter off his head.

"Oh Jesus God," the fisherman moaned.

"Shut up," Wolfe snapped.

"Yes, sir."

"Get out of here. And I suggest you go that way and keep going. You can do whatever you want, of course, but if you want to come back here and make a try for us in the dark, we will be right here. Feel free to try me anytime you like. Do you understand me?"

"Yes, sir." The fisherman bobbed his head some more.

"What about you?" Wolfe asked sweatshirt. "Do you want any more trouble?"

"No, sir, not me." Sweatshirt averted his eyes from Wolfe and Reba Crane. He stood aside while the fisherman pushed the cart with ball cap draped into it.

"Good. Go on now," Wolfe ordered.

The trio took the grocery cart and rolled off down the road, leaving one loaded cart behind, the one that held their plunder.

Wolfe quietly slipped through the night behind them long enough to satisfy himself that they were really going, then he turned back toward the camp. "Sorry. I guess our little celebration was ruined."

Reba shivered and said, "What you did...I never saw anything like it. And the other night, when you rescued me from those men, it was dark. I couldn't see your face so well that time. Now, even knowing you, knowing you wouldn't hurt me, I was scared. Your expression...I never saw anything like that. It was...I'm sorry but it was frightening. You were like some wild animal or something. All fury. And so terribly fast and powerful."

"I wouldn't hurt you," Wolfe said.

"I know that. Really I do but," she shook her head. "I'm sorry, Mr. Wolfe, you frightened me."

"You could call me Jim, you know."

Reba shuddered and mutely shook her head. No, he thought, the celebration was over. He walked over to collect the handguns the three men had been carrying but quickly shied away from them when he felt a tingle of radiation. Instead of claiming them he used a stick shoved through their trigger guards to pick them up and fling them away. Then he walked a little distance away so Mrs. Crane could have the comfort of the fire without his scary presence to bother her.

This newfound strength and quickness and fury were useful he reflected. Twice they had saved his bacon but they came at a price and it was a price he would have to pay whether he wanted to or not. Wolfe sat at the base of a large tree and stared off in the direction the scavengers had gone. He doubted they would come back but he intended to be prepared if they did try to sneak up on them.

In the morning Mrs. Crane found him and handed him the last piece of their unspoiled meat. Grouse, he thought. He hadn't thought they had grouse here but then he knew little about Idaho apart from its highways and a few truck stop waitresses.

"Thank you," he said. The woman looked sad this morning. She seemed to be in deep thought about something. She walked off into the bushes and spent a little time there taking care of business then returned and cleaned her hands by using clean soil as an abrasive substitute for water. He knew you can clean dishware like that but it never occurred to him that you could do the same for your hands. When she was finished she gave him a slow searching look and then said, "I want to apologize."

Wolfe blinked behind his protective pantyhose eye shield.

"I'm sorry for how I behaved last night. I was quite silly, Mr. Wolfe. I mean Jim. Will you forgive me?"

"There's nothing to forgive. A person doesn't choose to be

frightened, and I frightened you. I am the one who should be apologizing, not you.

"No, I was silly and I know it and I'm sorry."

Wolfe shrugged. "It doesn't matter."

"Oh, it matters, Jim. I owe you so much and so do my husband and my boy. They don't know that yet, but they will and when you meet them they'll tell you so themselves. After all you're the one who gave me back hope, got me away from the marauders and now you're helping me to get home where I belong.

"I'm not doing anything special, Mrs. Crane." She lifted an eyebrow and he smiled. "Excuse me. Reba."

"Much better. Thank you, Jim."

"Tell me about your family," he suggested. It was her turn to smile. The expression softened her features. He could see how she must have looked when she was a girl.

"I have never loved anybody else, Jim. I never was with anybody but my Harlan until...until recent if you know what I mean."

He nodded.

"We're just regular folks. Not rich but we never took charity from nobody. Harlan is a driller, water wells and like that. When there isn't work...I suppose I should say when there wasn't drilling work, there isn't any now of course, he would turn his hand to mechanic or whatever else was available. We always had food and love in our house. We raise a few chickens, little things like that.

She was smiling now but tears were running unheeded down her cheeks at the same time as she thought about home and the family who was still there. "I'll never be able to repay you for what you are doing, Jim. Not ever."

Wolfe said nothing but his thoughts were on Lurleen and Jojo. He could feel a hot rise of unshed tears in his own eyes at the memory of them and the worry for them that laid cold and hard behind those tears.

"We'd best be getting on now," he said, his voice gruff and hard. Somehow though, he did not think he was fooling Reba Crane by that. He only wished he could fool himself into forgetting, if only for a little while.

CHAPTER ELEVEN

I f it had not been for the darn pantyhose he would have
seen them. Wolfe was convinced of that but then if it
were not for the pantyhose he would not be able to see at all
during daylight hours. Even so the mask limited his vision all
too much and so he was not able to spot the men who were
waiting in ambush.

Wolfe and Reba had not walked more than five miles the
next morning from the place where ball cap and the others
had found them. Reba pulled the light weight and nicely
balanced bicycle cart while Wolfe pushed the much more
heavily laden grocery cart abandoned by the scavengers the
night before. The cart held what Reba said were absolute
treasures—five cartons of Winston cigarettes and two cans of
lighter fluid, a dozen packs of disposable razors, three small
cans of Prince Albert pipe tobacco, several dozen cans of
food with the labels missing and a package containing four C
cell flashlight batteries.

Wolfe could not see anything particularly exciting about
the articles but Reba assured him they were the next thing to

being priceless in the clear area. Two packs of cigarettes will buy you a bicycle tire, she explained as they walked along the highway and two cartons would buy you the bicycle. And bicycles are more valuable than gold.

It was no longer possible to buy gas for civilian use so travel nowadays was limited to how far you could walk, she explained, unless you have a job with transportation.

"That is, if you're working, like on the border fence they send a bus. They don't seem to have any problem finding gas for themselves," she said, sounding more than a little bitter. She frowned and added, "The people who raised horses before the war think of themselves as millionaires now, those of them who can keep the horses from being stolen and stay alive themselves while doing it."

"Crime is bad in the clear area too then?" Wolfe asked.

"Nothing as bad as it is here but it's bad enough. Livestock are stolen but mostly to slaughter. It isn't quite so bad with the horses because they're recognizable and if somebody does steal one how's he going to get away with it? I mean where can he go? He can't put it on a truck and haul it away like they used to so the horses aren't quite so vulnerable except for rustlers who already have horses and can get a pasture and drive the stolen stock out of the county. If they can make it outside walking distance they're pretty much home free. FEDCOM doesn't bother itself with that sort of policing."

"Can't they just get on a horse and ride away?"

"In theory sure, but if you see somebody carrying a saddle that is not on a horse you tend to get suspicious. Guys get shot for rustling just on suspicion of it, even if he isn't one."

Wolfe shook his head. "Horses, rustlers, it sounds like something out of a Western movie."

"In a way you could say that we have gone back to frontier days." Reba said.

"What about electricity and things like that?"

"It depends on where you are. Most places get none at all. Some places, like in areas served by a water generator...I forget what you call that."

"Hydroelectric," Wolfe suggested.

"That's it yeah, anyway if there's that hydra stuff power you might get electric part of the day. I don't know of anybody that has electric all the time. Radio, television, no TV. There isn't any anymore. There's one radio station, it's a government station run by FEDCOM. It gives news and sometimes music too but I don't know how believable the news is. I mean it isn't as if there is anything to compare it to."

"What about...?" He heard a clatter of rocks and a shout from behind a shed that was beside the road and in better times had been a school bus shelter.

Two men with guns stepped into view there and on the other side of the road was another pair. The one man who was not armed was the fisherman from the previous evening. That surprised Wolfe. If either of the survivors would have had enough gumption to try to retaliate against him he would have expected it to be sweatshirt. There was no sign of him though, just the seemingly timid fisherman and three strangers.

Wolfe felt naked and helpless. He had the bow, but it was lying in the cart and even if he could reach it there was no way he could nock an arrow on the string. On his person where he could reach in a hurry he had no weapon that could be used at anything more than arm's length. But then even if he did, there were four of them, three with guns while he was alone except for Reba. He almost wished he had kept one of those pistols despite the radiation danger. He was almost as angry with himself as with fisherman and his new friends.

Wolfe took his hands slowly off the push bar of the grocery cart and raised them over his head.

CHAPTER TWELVE

Fisherman was courageous but not until after Wolfe's hands were tied. Or he seemed to think he was with the three strangers holding Wolfe and Reba at gunpoint.

Fisherman produced a hank of clothesline and yanked Wolfe's arms behind him and proceeded to tightly bind Wolfe's wrists together. Once he was sure Wolfe could not hit him, fisherman tripped Wolfe, sending him tumbling painfully onto the pavement.

"You should not have messed with us, mister," Wolfe warned.

"You're not so tough now," fisherman crowed. He took the bowie knife from Wolfe's belt and used it to cut the free end of the rope. He used the rest of the clothesline to tie Reba then he removed the sheath from Wolfe's belt and threaded it onto his own then shoved the big knife back into it. Giving his captives a look of malevolent satisfaction, the fishermen kicked Wolfe in the ribs hard, then kicked him again.

"Hey, are you about done with him?" one of the gunman said.

"Yes. For now. It's about time he gets his comeuppance."

"Forget him for right now. Finish tying that woman. We don't want her running off someplace." The man laughed. "She's gonna be useful."

Fishermen grudgingly turned his back on Wolfe and took Reba very roughly by the arm, yanking her almost off her feet as he dragged her over to the bus shelter and pushed her into it.

Wolfe could not see what the fisherman was doing in there but perhaps that was just as well. The others could not see either and apparently that did not sit too well with them. They crowded close, one of them saying, "Be patient, you'll get your turn when we're done."

Two of them went to the shelter to check on fisherman and Reba while the third stood over Wolfe with a rifle. It looked like a .22 but that was enough to kill a man.

He aimed the rifle in Wolfe's general direction. His attention, though, was on the school bus shelter. After a few minutes one of the gunmen and fishermen returned. The newcomer took possession of the grocery cart and culled through the contents.

"Was I right or not?" fishermen asked. "It's all yours. All I want is the old guy." He paused for a moment, apparently in thought, then added, "And maybe those smokes. But I get the man, right? Him and that woman in there, they got my partners so I want them."

Partners, as in more than one, Wolfe noticed. The last he saw, sweatshirt was just fine except for a broken arm. If sweatshirt was dead now, fisherman had done it. For the contents of his cart probably, Wolfe suspected.

He noticed there was no sign of the cart fisherman and sweatshirt had taken with them last night. He guessed fisherman had hidden those from his newly acquired allies. He needed their help and their guns to get Reba and Wolfe and some of the cigarettes ball cap had been carrying. Now fisherman had it all. Or so he thought.

"You don't get my damn cigarettes," one of the gunmen said. "That was the deal. You can have everything else but we agreed I get two cartons of smokes. That's what you said." The man with the gun gave fishermen a baleful look.

"I just want things to be clear," fisherman said. "I want…"

"Billy, shut him up," one of the men said.

The gunman swung the barrel of his rifle away from Wolfe, and the .22 spat, the sound of gunshot sharp and nasty. Fishermen's look was of shocked disbelief. The small caliber slug caused no visible damage. There was no blood and the bullet hole was lost in the pattern of fisherman's shirt front, but his face drained of color until he was deathly pale. After a few moments he began to sway and crumble. His knees buckled. He caught himself once and managed to stagger upright, but the knees gave out again and he dropped slowly onto them. He raised a hand and gently, very tenderly touched the place low on his chest where the little bullet must have entered.

"You said…said …but you said…" With a wistful look almost like he was about to cry, fisherman doubled over, face forward on the ground. He continued moving for only a little while then his legs convulsed in a series of abrupt, shaky spasms. After that he did not move again.

"What do you think, Bert? Should I kill this guy here? Or should we bother wasting a round on him? You want me to cut him loose or something?"

"You want we should just leave him tied up here and take the woman with us? I'm not so sure we should just leave him here."

"Not so long ago you were going to shoot him. Now you're worried about his health. Make up your mind." Billy looked down at Wolfe who was staring up at him. Billy shrugged again. "Sorry, mister. You'll understand this, right? But don't worry. I'll make it quick and easy on you. Do you want to look the other way for me?"

Wolfe shook his head.

"Up to you, I guess. Just don't blame me."

Wolfe continued to glare at the scavenger. Billy was the one who turned away and headed in the direction of the school bus shelter.

CHAPTER THIRTEEN

It was the middle of the afternoon before the wilders left. They trussed Reba up with more of the clothesline, securing her hands behind her and tying the rest of the rope around her neck like a leash to lead her with then gathered up their own backpacks plus the bicycle and grocery carts Wolfe and Reba had had. The three men ignored the fisherman who lay dead on the pavement and Wolfe who lay hogtied beside him.

Wolfe did not like the look he saw on Reba Crane's face when the wilders led her away from the bus shelter. She appeared to be dispirited, without hope or promise.

She did not so much as glance in his direction. It hurt him to realize that. He had let her down. He knew it and so obviously did she. She was right to feel that way, he thought. For just that little while she had had hope. He gave her that, now had allowed it to be taken away. Much worse than that, though, was the terrible realization that his own dear Lurleen could be in a similar situation.

Even if she was still alive, and he prayed constantly that she was, she would surely be living in a Red Zone. Probably all of Florida had been subjected to intense radiation and much of it to bomb damage directly. Up one side of the state and down the other there was one military reservation after another. Important ones. And Central Command, just a few miles of open water from Bradenton was surely one of the most important installations in the country after the Pentagon and that mountain redoubt in Colorado where all the radar tracking was centralized.

He thought for a moment trying to remember the name of that one. It came to him after a bit. Cheyenne Mountain. He shuddered. If he let Reba Crane down how could he expect someone else to help Lurleen and Jojo if wilders or some scavengers wanted them.

He wanted—no, he needed—to take Reba safely home to her family and please God perhaps someone somewhere would do as much for his family.

Wolfe looked around as best he could manage and tried to concentrate on the here and now. Wilders and Reba too for that matter obviously regarded Wolfe as being already as good as dead. Unless someone happened by to release him from his bonds he would surely lie there until a slow and agonizing death claimed its victim of thirst, hunger and exposure.

Except Wolfe was not yet dead nor was he willing to meekly accept the ultimate failure. He had survived a nuclear holocaust so why should a little thing like this stop him now.

The men took their loot and their captive down the road to the south. Wolfe watched them out of sight then struggled to raise himself to a sitting position. He scooted sideways until he was beside the fisherman's body then twisted around until his back was to him. His hands were tied but he still had some feeling in them.

The fisherman had taken Wolfe's bowie knife just before he was killed. If Wolfe could lift the body a little and roll it over onto its back he should be able to reach the knife and cut himself free, he reasoned.

The position was an awkward one and he had lost part of the feeling in his hands but he was able to take hold of fisherman's belt, then lift and push. A sound very much like a groan escaped from fisherman when his body position changed. Wolfe understood that it was only discharge of gases in the man's final breath but it gave him a spooky, skin crawling sensation when he heard it anyway. He shivered despite the warmth of the sun on his shoulders and felt a momentary reluctance to touch the body again. Still he had no choice about it. He had to get to that knife.

He felt along fisherman's belt. He found nothing. The knife must be on the other side, he thought. Slowly Wolfe pushed with his legs and scooted on his backside down the length of the body, around fisherman's booted feet and then up the other side. But there was no knife on that side either nor had there been at the back of his belt and buckle which, Wolfe saw, was undone.

Probably one of the others must have seen the knife and taken it. Wolfe hadn't noticed. Cursing himself, angry with them and with fisherman and himself as well, Wolfe sat there on the roadway beside the dead man.

He had no idea how long he sat there like that, discouraged and unsure before his chin came up and he lifted his face toward the sky. A cold sense of resolution filled him, rolling into and through him like fog sliding over a hilltop and filling the valley below.

He would not die here. He would not. The thought was unacceptable and he refused to give in to it.

Wolfe felt the strength rise within him and course through his veins and muscles and sinews. He felt his shoulders swell and a prickle at the back of his neck. Hard muscles corded in his arms and across his shoulders. He clenched his fists and felt the power expand within him. No mere dime store rope could contain power like that. Probably chains would not have contained him.

Wolfe threw his head back and howled at the sky. With a mighty surge of effort he burst the bonds that held him captive. He took hold of the rope that bound his legs and snapped it in two then he leaped to his feet with a defiant roar. Wolfe was free and God help the men who had thought to destroy him. He began to trot, swift and tireless, in the direction where he last saw the wilders and their captive Reba Crane.

CHAPTER FOURTEEN

He went only a mile or a little more before he had to stop and consider a two lane county blacktop that crossed the state highway, the smaller road running east-west while the highway was north-south.

The wilders could have gone in any of three directions and if Wolfe chose wrong they would get farther ahead while he was looking in the wrong direction. They would not get away from him. Wolfe swore that to himself. They would not. But for Reba's sake, for her family's sake and in some manner he felt it would be for Lurleen's sake, he wanted to catch up with them as quickly as possible.

Their backpacks had been heavy with looted material scavenged from the Red Zone and now they had the grocery cart and bicycle cart too, loaded with things that Reba said were immensely valuable. They could be heading back toward the Clear Area now and that, he understood, was in Wyoming.

He turned to the left, toward the east, and resumed his run. An hour later he caught up with them. Wolfe stepped off the side of the road and stood behind the screen of thin brush while he considered what lay ahead. What he could see from there, several hundred yards distant were the two carts parked on the fringe of the road. The scavengers had to be within a few feet of those. They would not leave their treasures unguarded.

He glanced toward the sky. There was perhaps an hour of daylight remaining. Concern about Reba's comfort made him want to approach them as quickly as possible but that would be worse than foolish; it likely would be fatal.

It was still broad daylight and the three men were armed and he was not. Just as bad, his vision was impaired behind the fold of Reba's pantyhose. He still believed he missed seeing the men to begin with because of that poor vision. It was a mistake he did not intend to repeat.

Besides, come nightfall he would have the advantage of being able to see with complete clarity while they were the ones who would be nearly blinded by the poor light. Better, he thought, to wait here until it was dark and the men asleep. In the meantime he needed some sort of weapon. He poked around in the brush wishing there were blown down trees here but they had traveled far enough from the direct effects of the blast that there were fewer and fewer pockets of fallen timber. There were rocks aplenty but he did not regard them as useful weapons, not against firearms. Stone would be simply too hard to handle.

What he needed, he decided, was a club. It occurred to him that civilization had degenerated rather far in these past few months. Here he was, a modern man, reverting to the Stone Age in his attempt to stalk three other men. Wolfe was appalled that he could become so callous so quickly that he would deliberately seek to take a human life now. Three lives actually. And yes, he decided, yes those men committed murder. Not that the fisherman was anyone to grieve over but even so he was dead now at the hands of these scavengers. And then there was Reba.

Wolfe did not know, did not want to know the treatment she had received from them today. The only thing he needed to know about that was that he was responsible for her being in this situation. He was responsible now. There was no getting around it and that responsibility could not be denied.

If he went into that camp tonight with feelings of remorse or reluctance when it came to the three men and what had to be done to them, then he would fail again.

Wolfe continued searching the ground for a fallen tree limb that he could use as the equivalent to a war club of sorts. And come to think of it, there was no reason why he could not affix his pocket knife to the end of a longer limb to create a spear. That thought almost made him laugh. A club and a spear. He was becoming quite the savage. But that idea did not stop him from pursuing his savage mission. He continued to search for just the right weapons.

CHAPTER FIFTEEN

Wolfe pushed the strips of pantyhose off his eyes, wearing it like a headband holding his hair in place. It was a relief to be able to see clearly again without the thin mesh interfering.

He held a thick chunk of old cedar fence post in one hand serving as a club and in the other carried a six-foot length of sapling that would have to do as a spear. The only tip it had was the one he whittled down to as sharp point as he could manage. He just had not been able to figure out how to affix his folding knife onto the end of the shaft. What he wouldn't have given for a roll of good old duct tape; he grumbled silently as he walked softly on the fringe of the road.

It was several hours past full dark and he had neither seen nor heard anything from the scavengers' camp since dusk when he saw a little smoke rising from a culvert farther along the blacktop road.

Wolfe figured they must have their camp under the cover there. It should be a comfortable enough spot as long as it did not rain and there was no sign of that in the night sky. He moved up the road walking lightly and silently to a position from which he could observe the carts and the entrance to the culvert. The carts were parked directly above the concrete culvert which looked to be about five feet in diameter.

Wolfe did not know the name of the man who was posted as guard so presumably Billy and the one named Bert were inside the culvert sleeping while the third man guarded their treasures. That one, Wolfe remembered, had very little facial hair which made his beard and mustache wispy and rather silly looking. There was nothing silly about the rifle that lay across his lap, though.

Wolfe looked the situation over then backed away from the culvert as stealthily as he arrived. Once he was sure he was far enough away from the guard so he would not be seen he crossed over to the north side of the road and once more made a slow, silent approach to the culvert.

As he expected there was no guard on that end of the huge drainage pipe. Wolfe grimaced. Was there something about the criminal mind that required stupidity as a necessary ingredient? Not that he was complaining.

He was a little concerned that there might be too little light inside the culvert even for his unnaturally acute night vision and he worried a little too that once he was in there he would be silhouetted against the starlet night. If the two men were awake and happened to look toward that end of the culvert…Still, standing around worrying about things was not going to get Reba freed.

He slipped carefully through the ditch, creeping noiselessly to the open end of the culvert then stopped to listen. He heard neither voices nor movement from inside. The men, he guessed, would be twenty or thirty feet away and feeling secure in the protection of the guard at the other end.

With a scowl and the steeling of his resolve, Wolfe hefted the club in his hand until he was comfortable with its balance and grasped the spear shaft as well. He bent low and stepped into the mouth of the culvert where his enemies waited.

CHAPTER SIXTEEN

Wolfe felt a chill of apprehension. There were only two people asleep inside the culvert, only three sleeping bags laid out and one of those was empty obviously belonging to the man who was on guard at the far end. There was no sign of Reba Crane. Wolfe's hopes were dashed that he would be able to take her and slip away while the men slept.

Surely they would not have killed her. Besides he really thought he would have found her body if for some reason these men had murdered her. Wolfe was determined to find Reba alive, which he hoped for, or dead. Either way he intended to find her and for that he would have to ask one of these men.

He stepped lightly forward until he was standing over the nearer of the sleeping pair. It was the one called Bert. Wolfe nudged the man in the back of the head. He placed a hand over the man's mouth and cautioned him to silence as Bert stirred and came awake.

"No noise," Wolfe whispered.

The warning went unheeded as Bert grunted loudly and reached for a pistol that lay beside his head.

Wolfe had no choice. He had to quiet the man and he had to do it immediately or he would be finding himself facing at least two men with guns and possibly a third as well. Without taking time for conscious thought he lashed out with his club, the blunt end of the makeshift weapon impacting the sleeper's head with a sound like a ripe melon being dropped on hard ground. The shape of his head and face distorted and elongated as the skull shattered and flattened.

The sight sickened Wolfe but he had no time to worry about it for the other one who had been sleeping inside the culvert came awake and sat groggily upright. It was the one whose name Wolfe did not know instead of Billy who Wolfe was expecting to find.

When he looked at the guard from a distance, Wolfe had not seen clearly or they had changed the guard during those minutes while Wolfe was on the other side of the road making his approach to the culvert. Whatever this one's name, he too slept with a gun close at hand and he reached for it now.

Rage and power surged wildly through Wolfe engorging his muscles and giving him speed and strength beyond anything he ever imagined. Snarling like a wild thing, Wolfe attacked the wilder. The sharp tip of his spear shot forward with the speed of a striking viper. The wooden shaft drove deep into the underside of the man's jaw and on to invade the brain cavity itself. The man was dead before he would have had time to register his own pain.

Wolfe snatched the spear free of his enemy. Tossing his head back he howled loudly, the sound high-pitched and overwhelming inside the close confinement of the concrete road culvert. Wolfe felt the rush of primitive joy at this conquering of an enemy.

He raced to the entrance where Billy was on his feet peering nervously into the mouth of the culvert which to him probably was pitch black, its shadows impenetrable to his vision.

At the moment Wolfe gave no thought at all to the dangers of charging a man with a gun when he himself held only a club and the spear. He had no fear, only rage.

Despite the warning of Wolfe's howl, Billy was totally unprepared for the terrifying apparition that materialized out of the Culvert and flew out howling, snowy white hair flying wildly.

Billy stood immobile as if paralyzed by his own fear. He held his rifle at the ready but made no attempt to raise it or fire at Wolfe. He was too slow to turn aside the club that crashed down on the barrel of the rifle and on Billy's hand that happened to get in the way. The rifle clattered to the ground and Billy screamed with pain.

"Oh no, please man, please." Billy dropped to his knees clutching his broken hand with his good one. "Please." That last came out as a whisper.

Wolfe took hold of Billy's hair, tangling his fingers into it and as easily as if Billy we're a cardboard cutout of a grown man picked him up and held him aloft, his feet hanging a good six inches off the ground.

Billy screamed again and his face twisted as if he were going to cry. "Mister, please don't hurt me please."

Wolfe snarled, "Where is the woman?" He shook Billy back and forth.

The man squealed, "Mister, I swear to God I don't know where she is right now."

"You three took her with you. What did you do with her?"

"We traded her," the obviously terrified man said.

"What do you mean traded her?"

"I mean just that, mister. We was on our way back home. Your vehicle had enough stuff in addition to ours so we was going home, and we couldn't take no slave woman into the Clear Area. The damn feds would be all over us. We talked about staying out for a few more days to, you know, do whatever with her. Then Bert figured we could get rid of her before we went back inside the Clear but then we run across some fellas. You know. Scavengers like us. So we traded the woman to them. We got some salt for her and a couple of nice knives and a hatchet. I mean, why not? You know? At least it's something for her instead of killing her ourselves and getting nothing."

Wolfe gave the man a shake. "These scavengers, where were they going and how many of them were there? What do they look like? I want you to tell me, boy. I want you to tell me everything." Wolfe shook him again, Billy's feet and legs flopping around like those of the marionette held above the stage.

"I'll tell you, I will, just set me down please this…you're killing me. Please."

"If you tell me everything you know, boy, I won't kill you. Hold anything back, anything at all, and I'll crush your skull like I did your friend in there."

Billy was crying now. "I'll tell you, mister. Everything. I swear."

Wolfe set Billy down and stared at him waiting while Billy, babbling, sobbing, and shaking from his terror began to speak.

CHAPTER SEVENTEEN

"Mister, I told you everything I can remember. Honest."

"All right, now shut your mouth and sit there."

"You won't hurt me? You promised."

"I won't kill you," Wolfe told him again, "unless you move off that spot but if you stand up or try to crawl away all bets are off. Do you understand me?"

"Yes, sir. I won't do nothing I swear."

Wolfe believed him. Billy was thoroughly terrified and obviously believed that obedience was his only chance to avoid Wolfe's wrath. Giving Billy a final glance of warning, Wolfe turned and went back into the culvert. He retrieved two of the sleeping bags. The third was ruined, soaked with the blood of the slain man.

Wolfe recovered his bow and knife as well. He found and appropriated a flight bag containing the collection of knives, none of which seemed to have been contaminated and a Boy Scout hatchet. He was overjoyed to find a folding saw and dropped that into the bag along with the knives and hatchet.

All the firearms gave off the tingle of radiation except a

single action .22. There were only seven cartridges for that. No wonder they had been so reluctant to waste ammunition when they shot fisherman and then thought about shooting Wolfe too.

Wolfe took the assorted weaponry and sleeping bags and all the food he could find. He carried them up to the bicycle cart. He intended to keep that cart as it was light and nicely balanced and could be pulled with one hand.

When he went back down the embankment Billy was exactly where Wolfe had left him. "If you want to keep living stay exactly where you are and shut up."

"Yes, sir."

Wolfe went to the barbed wire fence that paralleled the county blacktop and carefully ran his hand close to the metal before accepting it as good since there was no tingling sensation coming off the wire. It occurred to him to wonder why he was able to feel radiation but no one else did or at least no one he had yet encountered. That was as mysterious to him as the changes in his sensitivity to light and the color of his hair and most of all the freaky strength he seemed to have after the two years inside the mine.

There was no way he could have held a grown man off the ground like that and kept him hanging there for so long without ever tiring. Wolfe did not understand any of this. All he could do was accept it.

He tugged at the strands of wire and chose the one that was most loosely attached to the cedar fence posts. He yanked it free. Several minutes of patient bending, folding the wire back and forth on itself weakened the metal and allowed Wolfe to break it apart.

He walked fifty or so feet down the fence line pulling the barbed wire free as he went and broke the strand again leaving him with fifty feet of old wire in his hands. He went back to where Billy waited.

"Get up. If you don't stand up I will get you up," Wolfe growled.

"Yes sir," Billy said.

Wolfe took him by the arm and dragged him inside the culvert. He doubted that Billy would be able to see much in the darkness there but he surely knew that Burt and the third man were dead. If nothing else he would be able to smell them. The culvert reeked with the copper scent of blood and the heavier fetid odor left when their bodies voided themselves in their death throes.

Billy stumbled and Wolfe hauled him upright, turning him around when he did so.

"Now stand still and put your hands behind you."

"Please don't…"

"Shut up. I'm going to tie you up. I don't trust you behind my back. After I leave you can try to free yourself."

"All right, sir all right." Billy was as cooperative as a puppy, holding his hands in place behind his back while Wolfe looped several extra tight wraps around them with barbed wire.

Wolfe could see the barbs digging into Billy's flesh but the frightened man made no complaint about the discomfort. Wolfe secured that end of the wire around itself then pushed Billy into a sitting position on the muddy culvert floor. "Don't move."

Billy said nothing, not even when Wolfe dragged first one of his dead companions and then the other and placed them beside Billy, propped up against his back. Then Wolfe took the free end of the wire and wrapped it tightly around each throat and around Billy's, finally around the third man's and then around Billy's again.

There was still a tail of ten or twelve feet of wire so Wolfe wrapped that around and around all three of them at throat level until he ran out of material.

"There," he said with satisfaction when he was done.

"How am I supposed to get out of this now?" Billy whined.

"When I've gone, feel free." Wolfe told him. "My money says you won't be able to do it and I'm betting you'll sit here until all three of you die and rot away, but you're welcome to try and get loose just like I promised. Now if you'll excuse me I have to go see if I can find Mrs. Crane."

Billy was still screaming the last Wolfe heard of him.

CHAPTER EIGHTEEN

He probably should have checked to see if any of the boots those men were wearing would fit him. His boots were holding up well so far but they would not last forever. Although they were what he had and would just have to do until he could find replacements.

He ran at a swift jog, setting as fast a pace as he thought he could maintain. Wolfe guessed the scavengers who held Reba were headed west intending to hit one of the major north-south roads and then move down to see if there was anything worth taking from the towns that lay north of the great Salt Lake and Salt Lake City.

The population in this vicinity had not been huge to begin with and apparently bands of scavengers and wilders had already picked things over pretty thoroughly.

Wolfe wanted to cover as much ground as he could during the night when his vision was unimpeded. During the day he had to keep his eyes covered by the layers of pantyhose mask and that made it difficult for him to make out details. He did not want to miss finding Reba because of poor eyesight.

He reached a crossroads that turned off his original route and paused. He knew the band had not gone north from there because he came down that road and had not passed them. He could be almost as certain they had not gone east toward distant Wyoming or there would have been no point in making the trade with the four men Billy claimed now held Reba, but if they wanted to pick over the houses and the stores north of Salt Lake City it would make more sense to continue south from here rather than going on toward the west before dropping down unless there was some particular place where they thought they might find loot.

Still it made no sense that they would make things more difficult for themselves by moving west from here.

He stood in the cool night air looking down one empty highway then the other trying to decide if Billy lied to him. He might have out of pure meanness and a desire to put something over on his tormentor. There was no way to know for sure. Not yet.

Wolfe made his guess and resumed jogging along the road Billy claimed the men were following. They might well have their reasons for taking the long way around. They might know of a backwoods community or isolated crossroads that they thought they could be the first to scavenge or for that matter they might be planning to meet someone up ahead so they could travel in a larger pack more secure with numbers.

The wilders would have to strike a delicate balance when it came to manpower. They needed enough strength either by way of weaponry or sheer numbers and perhaps with both so that they would not be vulnerable to attacks by the wrong kind. But if they had too many men the spoils of their thievery would have to be divided too many ways. It was a problem Wolfe was glad he did not have.

The mere thought that there were men evil enough to prey on their own kind was disgusting to him. He had no idea if Salt Lake City had been nuked. Probably it had but it was possible scavengers were expecting large numbers of survivors there who would be competitors in their search for the everyday items that were now treasures back east in the Clear Area.

Wolfe ran on into the night and as he ran he lifted his eyes momentarily toward the heavens and breathed a silent prayer that he would be able to find Reba and return her to her home and family. Her family and his had become twined in his mind. It was as if he had to prove himself worthy of returning to Lurleen by returning Reba to her family. Illogical as that might seem he could not shake the feeling that it was so, and the more the thought burned in him, the more determined he became to find Mrs. Crane and take her home.

CHAPTER NINETEEN

He woke to the bright light of afternoon. He had the pantyhose shield pulled over his eyes and a windbreaker draped over his head. Even so, the sunshine that was visible beneath the edges of the jacket seemed unpleasantly bright. The sensible thing, he supposed, would be to stay where he was, with his eyes thoroughly protected until nightfall when proper vision would return. Except every moment he stayed here the men who held Reba were moving farther away and Wolfe was not yet certain which direction they had taken at the crossroads back there.

By pushing himself through the night he managed to cover probably twenty miles. If he had to backtrack that would be forty miles and far too much time wasted while the scavengers went on their merry way.

The only good thing about this was that they would have no idea that they were being hunted. And there was no mistake about that. Wolfe was hunting them. He intended to bring them down. Hard if need be. He was determined to free Mrs. Crane from them.

He was responsible for the situation she found herself in

now and he would free her. There was no doubting that. He would free her.

Wolfe felt a chill race up his spine. The muscles across his shoulders went tense. He had heard something. The scrape of a shoe on gravel. A sigh. Something,

He reached up to make sure the eye shield was in place then dragged the windbreaker back from his forehead. He was not alone. He was surrounded by…it took a moment for his eyes to adjust to the light so he could count…at least six people.

There were four men and two women. They sat looking quite comfortable and at home on some fallen logs close to the tiny pond where Wolfe had stopped to make camp.

"Hello there old fella."

Old fellow, the stranger said. It was that thing with the white hair again, which Wolfe himself tended to forget about. Still, it could come in handy to be thought elderly. No one is afraid of the old and infirm.

These people that surrounded him while he slept certainly showed no concern. Wolfe sat upright and struggled to make some sense of this.

The men and the women too for that matter were all armed but they were making no threatening gestures. Their pistols were holstered and their long guns were laid aside.

"Are you hungry? We have enough to share," a middle-aged man offered. He had dishwater blonde hair and a beard. But then nearly every man seemed to have a beard nowadays, a change that Wolfe had not adjusted to yet.

"Who are you?" Wolfe said.

"Travelers," the fellow said. "Movers, you might say. Mind if I ask you something?"

"No, go ahead."

"What's a blind man doing out here all alone? Somebody run off and leave you to die?"

"No, it isn't like that." Wolfe was on the verge of admitting that he had sight, then realized that could be a mistake. He did not know who these people were or what they wanted. It might be better to withhold that information.

"Mind if I give you some advice?"

"Please."

"My guess is that you or somebody helping you can see at least a little bit, isn't that right?"

Wolfe nodded but he stopped short of telling him that he was alone. He was distracted for a moment by a lean woman with stringy hair but a gentle smile who leaned over him and pressed a plastic bowl and hastily whittled wooden spoon into his hands.

The bowl held a sort of stew that looked like it had been made with a can of pork and beans, some limp vegetables that looked like weed roots but smelled like onion and some pieces of mystery meat.

"You've laid out beside the only good water we've seen around here what with that spring feeding the pond. Stands to reason that man or animal this is the place they'd head toward so if you want to stay hidden, judging from the way you covered your cart over with those branches I'd say you were hoping not to be found. If you want to stay hidden, mister, you want to find your water and take what of it you want then move someplace else to bed down.

"I never thought of that," Wolfe confessed. He still had quite a bit to learn about life in the Red Zone. If he lived long enough to acquire the necessary lessons. These people with their weapons and superior numbers could cut his education short in a heartbeat if they chose to do so.

But the man who seemed to be leading the group only nodded and smiled. "Eat your supper, friend."

Friend. Wolfe hoped he could believe that. "May I ask you something?"

"Sure. We've got nothing to hide."

"I don't know which way you came but…"

"Up the road from that direction," the man said. We're all members of the same church congregation back home in eastern Colorado. We tried living in a Clear Area over in Kansas but we don't like the way the Federal Command wants to run everything and everybody. We are free Americans and intend to stay that way. Not that an American can be free nowadays so we decided to head into the Red Zone and see if we can make our way to Canada."

"Is it better up there?"

The man grinned "Darned if we know but it can hardly be worse and rumors say Canada wasn't involved in the fighting, at least not right at first, so maybe they're all right up there and Federal Command doesn't say. Which makes us think it might be better there and they just don't want the whole dang countryside picking up and moving north.

"You, um, you're church folks?"

The fellow laughed. "Do you mean are we going to rob you? No, we wouldn't do that but we might be interested in doing some trading if you like."

Wolfe nodded. "The thing I need most is information." He took a bite of stew. It was growing cold but tasted very good. He thought about asking what the fresh meat was but thought better of that. He probably was happier not knowing.

"Finish your supper, my friend, while we have ours, then we can talk. If there is any way we can help we'll be glad to."

CHAPTER TWENTY

The leader of the little group of travelers called himself Elder Johnson. The others were introduced by their first names only and obviously deferred to the elder for all group decisions.

"Four men and a woman, you say." Johnson shook his head. "No I haven't encountered any such group as that. Not in the past couple weeks anyway."

"This would have been in the past day," Wolfe said.

"No, not on this road."

Wolfe sighed. That meant he had chosen the wrong road back at the intersection where Billy told him he last saw Mrs. Crane. That gave the scavengers two, perhaps three days head start on him now. He had a lot of catching up to do.

"Is something wrong?" Johnson asked.

Wolfe explained the problem.

"That means you'll be traveling south from here. If you don't mind the warning, everything south of Ogden and Salt Lake City and of course to the lake itself would have to be considered off-limits. Those areas are saturated with radiation. We have a little battery-powered detector and a solar recharging unit that allowed us to avoid the worst hit areas. Since you don't have an instrument your best bet will be to stay as far east as you can go.

"There is a border fence for part of that distance so go all the way to it and walk parallel to the fence as close you can get. Even if there are FEDCOM guards they won't shoot you if you don't try to cross over illegally into the Clear Area."

Fences, guards, FEDCOM. "It's all so strange," Wolfe said. "It's almost as if I'm in a completely different country."

"Friend, indeed you are in a different place from the one you and I always knew before. That is why we are leaving it now although we hope someday we can come home and help make it our America again."

"Amen to that, elder," Wolfe echoed.

"A little while ago you mentioned something about trading. Were you serious about that?"

"Yes sir, I am."

The church leader grinned. "Would you care to display your wares, Mr. Wolfe?"

"Yes, sir, I'd be happy to, Mr. Johnson."

By the time night fell Wolfe was the pleased owner of four cans of Armor corned beef, two of Spam and six of Hormel Vienna sausages acquired in exchange for the knives he'd taken from Bert and Billy and the other wilder back at the culvert.

"We don't really mind giving up the canned goods," Johnson admitted, "because we have enough ammunition that we can provide for what meat we need by hunting along the way."

"You have a good bit of ammunition, do you? .22 caliber too? I have that rifle over there but only seven cartridges for it. I don't suppose you would consider swapping me some of your ammunition."

"Not a snowball's chance, as the saying goes. But I'd trade you a canned ham for that rifle. The only .22 we have is a revolver. A rifle would be of much more use to us. It's good ham. Danish."

"Two hams," Wolfe countered.

"We only have the one."

"One ham isn't much when the rifle would get me seven rabbits before my ammo was all used up."

Johnson thought about that for a moment. "We have two bicycle inner tubes. Those are in short supply and of value if someone has a bicycle. Which we don't."

"I don't have a bike either."

"No and the people who do have them treat them like gold. Valuable as bicycles are, the inner tubes would make good trading material."

It was Wolfe's turn to ponder. After a few moments he nodded. "All right, it's a deal."

"I would suggest that you try to fit yourself out with some sort of weapon, Mr. Wolfe. Something better than that bow. Bows are primitive weapons and these are dangerous times indeed."

"Yes sir, I'll do that first chance I get." He grinned and added, "Bad as I am at shooting a bow and arrow, don't think I can even consider it to be a weapon. Not quite yet anyhow."

Johnson smiled. "In the meantime another bowl of stew before you turn in for the night?"

"Thank you for the hospitality, but I'll be moving along. Now that it's dark I'll be able to travel more comfortably anyway."

"Of course. In the dark, so the wilders are less likely to see you passing by."

Wolfe never had gotten around to explaining about his eyesight and did not do so now. He just made the exchange of goods that they agreed upon and headed back up the road in the same direction he had just come from. He was as determined as ever to catch up with Reba and the men who now held her. It was going to take longer than he had hoped it might, that was all.

CHAPTER TWENTY-ONE

Wolfe paused at the crossroads where he had originally guessed wrong. He was tempted to keep going back as far as the culvert where he left the scavenger named Billy. He was feeling guilty now about leaving him tied in place like that, never mind that Billy was a murderer and rapist and God knew what else. A liar, that was for sure.

Billy lied about which direction the scavengers took Reba. If it had not been for that Wolfe surely would have caught up with them already. Despite that, though, if it had not been for his concern about finding Reba and freeing her, he very likely would have gone back to turn Billy loose. As it was, he just did not have time.

Maybe...he shook his head. There would be no other time. It was Billy's tough luck that Reba Crane's needs came before his. Even so Wolfe felt guilty about leaving him to die like that.

He turned and resumed his swift jog, this time moving south on the state highway he last covered from the comfort of his own cab with music anytime he wanted it. He surely did miss the radio and CD player and tape deck. At times they were the closest companionship he had.

He smiled a little as he ran. That was one difference between driving this route and jogging it. This way he could let his mind wander as far away as odd thoughts cared to take it. But this way was slower than he was used to.

His expression sobered and turned hard and he increased his pace, the bicycle cart rolling smoothly along behind him. He had miles to cover and his own life to get on with.

Two hours later he slowed to a gradual halt and once again stood at a crossroads. Wolfe stood there cursing under his breath for several minutes while he tried to assess the possibilities. From here there were three directions the four scavengers could have gone and Wolfe had no way to guess which they might have chosen. From here on it would be assumption and guesswork.

He had plenty of time to worry about it though. The coming break of day was turning the sky orange toward the east and already he had to pull one layer of black nylon over his eyes to shield them. He needed to find some place to get undercover so he could sleep and not be too vulnerable to attack.

There was a small house on the southeast corner of the intersection. Its doors and windows stood gaping empty. The place obviously had been ransacked many times over. That did not bother Wolfe. He was not there looking for loot. He only wanted a dark and fairly well protected place where he could sleep.

The open windows of the house, though, would mean the place would be flooded with daylight in another hour or less.

On the southwest corner sitting catty-corner to the two roads was an ancient service station from back in the days when gas stations really did give service and did not sell groceries. The place probably dated from the 1940s or even earlier. It was built of native stone with a concrete block addition to one side where a service bay was open to the elements. The single, antiquated gas pump probably had not seen active use for decades. It looked that old anyway although it did not look like it had been kept in good shape.

The garage stood on a wedge of gravel in front of both of the intersecting roads. There was a large hole where a window had been in the original stone part of the building. The glass was gone now and the door to this structure had been broken just like the house across the road.

Wolfe briefly wondered if the house had been owned by whoever operated the gas station and what might have happened to them.

Above the service bay doors a large, crudely lettered sign read 'welding.' A pair of large wooden doors stood wide open beneath the sign. Those doors, he thought, were intact. He could pull them shut and cut off most of the painful daylight and they would also hide both him and the bicycle cart from the view of anyone who might pass during the day.

Wolfe glanced toward the east where the light grew steadily stronger. If he wanted to push it he could make another mile or two before he stopped but he knew good and well he was not likely to find a better place to hole up than this one.

With a satisfied grunt he turned off the road and headed for the old service station to get some sleep.

CHAPTER TWENTY-TWO

Once he got inside with the double doors pulled shut he was able to take the strip of pantyhose off his head and see normally without the intervening mesh to soften everything and put an artificial fog over his eyes. Besides, it just plain felt good to be free of the constriction around his head.

Wolfe took a look around inside. The place had been ransacked of course, probably many times over by every group of Red Zone scavengers that passed by during the first months of shortages over in the Clear Area. After all the old service station sat at a highway crossroads and would have been passed by all manner of wanderers.

He supposed pretty much everyplace was considered fair game. Taking abandoned goods anywhere in the Red Zones would likely be considered simple common sense rather than looting. Wolfe had not quite yet made that adjustment in thinking but it did make sense. Whoever once owned these things left them behind and hurried to get away from the radiation poisoning of the bombs or, worse, they were dead now. Either way he supposed the ordinary property rights of the past no longer applied. Everything left behind belonged to whoever wanted it.

Not that so very much remained here in the service bay. A greasy, battered vehicle hoist occupied most of the floor space. It was a hydraulic lift powered by an electric pump and therefore was useless now.

Wolfe knelt and carefully ran his hands close to the welded steel but there was no tingle coming off any of the fixtures or equipment. He supposed the inside of the building had been protected by distance from the bomb blast and by the stone and concrete block construction and perhaps by wind direction as well. For whatever reason the contents of the station seemed free of radiation contamination.

He pushed his bicycle cart into a corner and grimaced before laying a sleeping bag over the chipped concrete. Layers of grit and grease several generations thick made the prospect unattractive but even so it beat going back outside into the sunlight.

He took a look around. The air hose had been cut off the electric compressor. The hose was gone, taken by someone who thought he might have a use for it, but the heavy compressor was intact. So was a 220 volt electric welder. The wires from it had been scavenged, perhaps for the copper content, but there were no welding rods in the rack that should have held them and the welding unit sat dark and useless at the back of the service bay.

Pale circles on the floor showed where something used be. It took Wolfe a moment, then he realized that probably was where the oxyacetylene welding tanks and hoses had been. That whole outfit had been carried away although most certainly not by anyone traveling on foot. The weight would simply be too much to lug by hand. It would take a sturdy cart or perhaps a horse drawn wagon to haul the tanks and accessories. Now all that remained of the welding gear were one twisted and flattened wire brush that had seen better days and a pair of grease crusted welding goggles lying overlooked behind the bulk of the electric welder.

Wolfe stepped into the small storage room, more a large closet than a room really, that was tucked in at the left rear of the bay. The shelves held air filters, fuel filter replacement cartridges and car and truck inner tubes but no lubricants of any sort, making it clear enough even if it hadn't already been that all of his ideas about private transportation were completely out of date in this topsy-turvy postwar world he found himself in.

Every hand tool that must have been in the garage was now gone, but the air powered tools remained, tossed aside as being useless now that there was no longer electricity to power the compressor or gasoline to generate electric.

Wolfe felt like a stranger in his own land. In a way he supposed he was. He took a look around the service bay then went to lie down to sleep through the day. The concrete was cold and unyielding through the entirely too thin layers of fabric in the sleeping bag, but he was tired enough that he doubted that would matter very much.

He smoothed his hair back off his forehead. Lord, what he wouldn't give for a plain old plastic comb right now, and pulled the nylon headband back in place on his forehead, carefully doubling and smoothing it so if he needed to be able to see during the day he could quickly put it into place.

He lay back with a sigh and thought that a pillow would be nice. He could probably find one inside an abandoned house if he stopped to look. A foam rubber pillow should not have gotten musty or moldy. He would have to look but not right away. His first order of business would be to catch up with those men and see what he could do to help Reba

Crane. That was the sort of thing he would think about tonight though, after he had some sleep.

He was tired now. Worn out. He closed his eyes and tried to will his muscles and mind into immobility. He began that slow, pleasant drift, spiraling down into sleep. Then sat bolt upright with his eyes wide open.

Dummy! He chided himself. *Why the heck didn't you think of that before now?*

Grinning, Wolfe leaped to his feet and hurried back to the corner of the filthy service bay.

CHAPTER TWENTY-THREE

Excitement was enough to push fatigue away. He grabbed the welding goggles and looked through them. They were dirty and layered with grease but the glass was intact and very dark. Even if they were badly scratched he realized they would be a far cry above the strip of Mrs. Crane's pantyhose for blocking sunlight.

With these he should be able to have normal daytime vision.

He washed the glass as best he could and the molded rubber the glass lenses were mounted in. The glass was still smudged so he cut a piece of flannel lining out of a sleeping bag and used the soft cloth to clean and polish both lenses.

"Perfect," he mumbled aloud. He adjusted the head strap and put the goggles on then took a deep breath and stepped rather fearfully outside.

From the moment he left the mine, daylight had been his enemy and a painful foe at that. But with the welding goggles to cut the light he had normal vision again.

Best of all because the goggles fit tightly against his face there was no stray light leaking in around the lenses the way there would've been had he been wearing sunglasses. Even wrap-around sunglasses would not do this good a job.

Wolfe felt revitalized by the find. He went back inside and closed the doors again then pulled the goggles down so they hung against his throat. He could push them into place in a second or two if need be and they were comfortable enough there.

They would need some getting used to but he was as happy with this find as if he had won a lottery. Well, a small one anyway.

Once again Wolfe lay down and tried to make himself comfortable on the hard concrete floor. Something was nagging at him, something he felt should have been obvious but was not. He shrugged. It would come to him. Maybe.

Wolfe had no idea how long he had been asleep. Several hours probably. He woke with a rush and sat bolt upright.

He thought he had heard or somehow sensed the approach of someone or something dangerous. He shoved the goggles into place and stepped into what once had been the service station office.

An old fashioned cash register that sat on a grimy, wooden desk had been broken into. The drawer hung at an angle off the edge of the desk. An ancient swivel chair with a foam rubber pad on the seat lay on its side.

The front window had been broken and there was no sign of the merchandise that had once been on the shelves. Bright yellow forms and several receipt books lay scattered on the floor.

Wolfe's interest was not what he might scavenge but in using the front room as a sort of listening post. He leaned against the front wall, out of sight if anyone was outside, but could hear nothing more threatening than the sighing of the breeze and the chittering of a squirrel somewhere nearby.

He chanced a look outside and was delighted to be able to

see with perfect clarity. He did not at all miss the foggy, fuzzy appearance given everything by the layers of nylon mesh.

He stood there watching and listening for some minutes before he remembered what it was that awakened him. Then, laughing out loud, he turned and went back into the service bay.

CHAPTER TWENTY-FOUR

He had seen some inner tubes in the storage room. He grabbed a pair of the flimsy boxes, opened one and tossed the other into the bicycle cart along with other left-overs from the civilized world that he was collecting there.

He was already learning that you never knew what might come in handy. Inner tubes, for instance.

Using the Bowie knife he sliced the inner tube in half close to the valve stem, then made another cut so the metal tube was eliminated. What was left was a doughnut-shaped tube of thick rubber.

He returned to the service station office and laid the tube out lengthwise on top of the wooden desk and began cutting again, slicing the rubber into long strips of slightly varying width from roughly three quarters of an inch to an inch and a half wide, each strip about two and a half to three feet long.

That should be long enough, he thought. If it wasn't he could always find a truck tube and cut something longer. But he thought these would work.

He tested the strength of the rubber strips and selected one a little wider than an inch.

All he needed now was a y-shaped yoke of a good, sturdy material. Metal, plastic, he didn't care about that. It just had to be strong enough to support a very strong slingshot.

As a boy, before he had been old enough to be trusted with a BB gun, he had thought of himself as quite the mighty hunter with a child-sized slingshot. Now he wanted a grown-up version of the weapon.

A slingshot was accurate enough at close range, silent, no flashes of flame to give him away in the night, all the advantages offered by a bow. And he felt more comfortable shooting a slingshot. He had had much more practice with one. Never mind how long ago that had been. And he should be more accurate with it.

The truth was, he was woefully inaccurate with the bow.

Even with the goggles that allowed him good vision in daytime, his natural element was night. And his best defense. Human enemy or animal prey, either one would be at a disadvantage in the darkness.

So it only made sense, he thought, to use a slingshot, a bow or a spear. And ammunition for a slingshot was inexhaustible. Any stone or pebble or small object would serve.

Wolfe threw his head back and laughed again. Any small, heavy object. Perfect.

He went into the storage room and emerged a moment later carrying a plastic, gallon jug with its top cut off. The label showed it once contained grape drink.

Wolfe would have been happy to enjoy a glass of grape drink but was just as happy to have the dozen or more lug nuts that the jug now contained.

Those would be perfect ammunition for a slingshot, small enough and heavy enough and would hit with one whale of an impact.

A lug nut fired at high speed would wound or even kill a human if it came to that.

He stashed the jug of lug nuts in the bicycle cart, which was loaded pretty much to capacity by now.

He looked around inside the service station for something he could use to complete the making of a first class, extra powerful slingshot.

There were any number of things he might have used. If he had a hacksaw that would allow him to cut the discarded electric or pneumatic shop tools apart.

A pistol grip would have been ideal. Except he had no way to cut away the body of a heavy drill, for instance. Nothing else in the station looked suitable either, so he pulled the goggles into place and trotted across the highway to the abandoned house.

The front door stood open on broken hinges and every window in the place had been shattered, but even so Wolfe felt like an intruder into someone's privacy as he entered. This was someone's home, or had been, and he felt he had no right to pry into their space nor steal their possessions.

He shivered when he entered, and it had little to do with the musty chill inside the abandoned house.

The furniture was still there, most of it smashed now, upholstery sliced open by malicious vandals who could not possibly benefit from their nastiness. They destroyed for no purpose.

Wolfe felt contempt for them. Why would they have destroyed the things that some family once held dear? Why in the world would they have shattered the picture tube of the old television set in the tiny living room? Wolfe did not understand such behavior. But then he did not really want to understand people like that.

He understood very well the people who must have lived here. The magazines scattered on the floor suggested they had been an older couple thinking of moving to Arizona or the Rio Grande valley when they retired.

They probably were Catholic, judging by the pictures on one wall. At least the vandals had left those alone, he noted.

The refrigerator was practically an antique, with the softly rounded corners that went out of style decades ago. The kitchen cabinets had been painted time after time yet still were chipped and battered and in need of painting again.

Except this time there would be no freshening up. No spring cleaning. No joy at the acquisition of new chairs for the dinette set or new curtains to brighten the windows.

Saddened by the wanton destruction he stood inside the dark, cluttered little bedroom that had been shared by whoever lived here. He offered up a silent prayer for the people he would never know. He hoped they were safe now, wherever it was they had fled.

After pausing for a few moments there he resumed his search through the house for the stout yoke he needed to complete the slingshot.

An hour later he was smiling as he trotted back across the empty highway to the service station, a snow shovel in his hand. Half an hour after that he was smiling even more broadly at the finished product he held.

A hatchet had chopped away the handle of the snow shovel, leaving a sturdy 'Y' of metal. More chopping cut away the blade of the shovel, leaving him with the makings of his new weapon.

After that he only needed to attach the rubber strips to complete the slingshot. A funny looking one, perhaps, but nonetheless, now he had the weapon he needed.

Wolfe stepped outside and squeezed a lug nut in the center of the rubber strip. He pulled it back as far as his arm length permitted and let fly.

The heavy steel nut soared a good dozen feet or so before it plopped tamely onto the gravel.

The thick, inner tube rubber was strong. And sturdy. And useless for making slingshots.

Once he gave it some thought it made sense. The inner tube rubber was not made for resilience but for strength. The slingshots he had as a boy were made of light, stretchy rubber.

A pal had a Whammo slingshot made with surgical tubing. That had been as powerful as a small pistol and was the envy of the entire neighborhood, Jimmy Wolfe included.

Inner tube rubber, though…He sighed. And went to the bicycle cart to unload the jug of lug nuts.

It had been a heck of an idea, though. He still thought it was.

He would have to get in some practice time with the bow, that was all. He would have to come up with something to make arrows once the original supply became lost or broken.

Wolfe yawned and stretched. He was wide awake now and anxious to be on his way again. He had gotten some sleep. Enough for the moment. He had to be on his way again if he hoped to catch up with the men who held Reba Crane.

As it was he felt bad about the time he had wasted making that darn slingshot.

Wolfe dragged the service bay doors open and knelt to roll up his sleeping bag and return it to the cart.

CHAPTER TWENTY-FIVE

Once again at this crossroads Wolfe had a one in three chance of taking the same road followed by Reba Crane's captors. Any route he picked could be the wrong one, wasting days or even weeks before he got back on their trail. But he had to try.

He would not forgive himself if he dropped the pursuit and went about his own business while Reba remained in harm's way. Besides, he at least had a choice. She did not.

He hesitated only a moment before making that choice. The scavengers seemed to be wanting to make their way south. He picked up the long, aluminum shaft of the bicycle cart and set off at a fast trot. It was a pace, he was discovering, that he could maintain hour after hour without needing to stop for rest. It might not be as fast or as comfortable as his tractor had been but it would do.

The farther south he went, the more smashed or disabled cars, pickups and trucks he found. And here, well out of the way of the Boise warhead and before he got into the Salt Lake City zone of destruction he was finding there was little to no evidence of radiation.

Every vehicle he came to had already been ransacked, of course, but most appeared simply to have run out of gas or broken down. At least there was seldom any visible damage.

Farther north most of the vehicles had been in accidents. He was guessing those had been caused by panic-stricken drivers whose judgment was destroyed…along with so much else. Or even by drivers who were blinded by the enormous fireballs.

Wolfe counted himself lucky to have survived. So far.

Whenever he paused, whether to rest or eat, he made sure he took a few minutes to practice with the bow. Slowly his eye and arm began to work together and by the afternoon of the second day after leaving the service station he was accurate enough to bring down a rabbit using his practice arrow, that being the most expendable if he should lose it in the brush or hit a rock and smash the shaft.

He cooked and ate in the late afternoon when the welding goggles would protect his vision from the bright light of the flames. Firelight after dark would be painfully bright and ruin his vision for some time afterward.

He ate, then kicked the fire apart and ran on for another several hours, until well after dark before he found a place to stop for the night.

A driveway and a bare post where a mailbox must once have been led him off the highway and past a cattle guard to a rambling, ranch style house surrounded by sheds, pens and small barns.

Wolfe approached the house cautiously. As he came nearer the hair on the back of his neck prickled and itched. He jumped nearly out of his skin when he heard a loud, sharp clang from somewhere to his right.

It was only then that he realized what it was about this place that made him nervous.

It was normal. That is, it was the way an isolated homestead might have been before the war. The clanging that he heard was the drop of a steel lid on a feeder and inside one of the pens he could see movement. Hogs. Several of them.

He could smell them too and realized now that the odors were fresh ones, not the dry, fading scents he had encountered at other places along the way.

The presence of hogs still alive inside a small enclosure meant they were being tended by someone.

Wolfe stopped in the middle of the farmyard and called out, "Hello. Is anyone here? Hello."

"Stand still," a voice came from the fringe of a woodlot to his left. "Now, step away from that cart thing and keep your hands away from it. Are you armed?"

"I have a bow," Wolfe admitted.

"What about your guns?"

"I don't have any guns on me."

"Well, I do. So just stay still. Wait there. I'm going to send one of my people out to look you over."

He heard a crackling sound as someone pushed his way through the underbrush and a man came into view. He was a thick-bodied man, balding and gray. His hands were empty of weapons, Wolfe noticed. That made sense. Probably the people here sent their weakest member, deliberately unarmed so an intruder could not snatch a gun away and attack them with their own weapon.

"Stand easy now, old fella. Let me look you over."

Wolfe was almost used to being mistaken for an old man by now, but something else about the comments bothered him. Then he realized. The voice was the same one that had called to him from the bushes to begin with.

Send out "one of his people" to look Wolfe over, would he? Wolfe began to wonder if there were any other people hidden from him.

That was answered soon enough when he saw two faces

appear beside a tall shrub. Two women. It was dark and they probably thought they could not be seen. Very likely they would have been correct except for Wolfe's altered night vision.

Wolfe obligingly stepped away from the cart so the man could look it over.

"I'm not armed and I don't have any hostile intent, mister."

"You got something in your belt there. Is that a gun?"

Wolfe frequently forgot that others could not see in the dark as well as he was able to. "No, sir. Just a knife."

"Hold it up. Let me see."

Wolfe did.

"All right. But mind, I'm going to keep my boys hid so they can cut you down if you try anything."

"Yes, sir." Wolfe doubted there were any boys, but the deception was understandable and he took no offense.

"Aggie. Darla. You can come out now. It's just an old fella passing through."

That was far from being accurate but Wolfe didn't argue the point.

"Are you hungry?" the farmer asked.

"No, sir. But I have a couple squirrels here if you'd like to add them to your pot."

The fuzzy-tailed rodents had come out just after dark to forage on the ground, and Wolfe had taken them at close range with the bow. Three shots, two squirrels. He thought that was doing pretty well. And he had not lost an arrow though the point of his practice arrow was becoming pretty battered.

"You're offering us food?"

"Sure."

"Mister, I don't think nobody's done that since the bombs

went off. Nobody in all the folks that have come by and asked us to feed them."

Wolfe smiled. "So, did you?"

"Did I what?"

"Did you and your family feed them?"

"Well, yeah. Mostly. There were a couple we ran off."

Wolfe laughed. "By pretending you had sons hidden over there?"

"I wasn't pretending."

"Friend, I can see your wife standing over there by that tree. And there's a younger woman, your daughter I'd be guessing, over there." He pointed. "All either one of them has in their hands are some short spears. You don't have any guns, do you?"

"Of course I got guns."

"Yes, sir. If you say so." Not that Wolfe believed it for a moment but it was all right with him if the gentleman wanted him to believe it was so.

"Aggie. There's two squirrels here. Skin them and take them into the kitchen, Darla honey. See what we can find for this gentleman to eat. Mister, you can come inside. But mind now, my boys will be laying out keeping watch on you."

"Yes, sir. Thank you."

CHAPTER TWENTY-SIX

"What in the world is this contraption?" Wolfe asked as the young woman passed him carrying his brace of squirrels.

The farmer grinned. "You never saw one of those?"

"No, sir. I surely never. It's what…a spear thrower of some kind?"

The article or weapon, he supposed it should be properly called, consisted of a thin, fairly short spear that was laid alongside a curved table leg with a socket at one end where the butt of the spear was fitted and the other end had been carved down to provide a hand grip. A thong made of braided twine was tied at the thin end and looped around Aggie's wrist so she would not drop it.

"Spear thrower would be one way to put it," the farmer agreed. "The proper name for them is an atlatl. Ancient Indians and such invented those before the bow. They multiply the leverage in a person's arm by extending it so you can throw the spear farther and harder than by just using your hand."

"I like that."

"Would you like one?"

"Oh, I couldn't."

"The throwing part came off a table and chair set in our neighbor's place a couple of miles over. The neighbor took off toward Boise after the first bombs went off. Haven't seen anything of them since, of course. If they had lived they surely would have been home by now."

"Why did you stay here?" Wolfe asked.

"We stayed hid out in the root cellar for a while. Came out twice a day to feed livestock and watch over things. Then we realized if we were going to get poisoned by the radiation we already would have done so. After a spell we moved back into the house. We haven't any of us been sick a day since so I guess it's all right here."

"Yes, sir, it is," Wolfe said with conviction. He hadn't encountered any of the tingling sensations anywhere within the past twenty miles or more.

"Know that for a fact, do you?"

"Yes, sir, I do," Wolfe said, nodding. "Did you have no trouble with the wilders and scavengers here?"

"We had trouble enough for the first few months but we were able to take care of ourselves. We really do have guns in the house. Of course we ran out of ammunition about five or six months back. That's why we have the spears and atlatls on hand. So far they've been enough."

"I would think everyone would be running out of ammunition before too long," Wolfe said.

"I hope so. In the meantime," the farmer shrugged, "we have our animals and enough cleared ground to raise a garden for ourselves and a little alfalfa and soybeans for the stock. Fortunately a pig will eat most anything you throw to it, including grass cuttings. The chickens take care of themselves mostly although we lose some to the hawks now and then. I just wish I had some way to get at them damn hawks…excuse my language but now that all our shotgun shells are gone I can't touch 'em. Shoulda known better than to waste shells on them to begin with, but I just couldn't stand watching them come down and kill my hens."

"How are you managing to plow?" Wolfe asked.

"Right now it's all spade and hoe work, but I have some implements that I think I can modify to pull with draft stock. And I have a pair of bull calves that will grow out to oxen in time. We're already training them to a yoke."

"You're doing all right, aren't you?"

"Better than the folks who come through here," the man said. He shook his head. "The stories they tell about the condition of things, it must be pretty bad, even over in the Clear Area where there's at least a little law and order. But folks there say they pay a high price for that. They say that Federal Command runs roughshod over everything and everyone. As for us, we'll be all right here as long as scavengers don't get us.'

"Come along to the kitchen now," the old woman said. "I have some leftover fried chicken you might like."

"Fried chicken. Good Lord." Wolfe's mouth began to water, literally flow heavy with saliva at the thought of something as civilized, and wonderful, as a piece of fried chicken. He wished Reba were here to have some too. She probably would be as excited by that as she would be by a Burger King Whopper.

"Would you like some eggs to go with that?" Darla asked. "And maybe a glass of buttermilk?"

Wolfe was fairly sure he must have died and gone to Heaven. Fried chicken? Fresh eggs? Buttermilk to wash it down with? Oh, my. He was a very contented fellow when he followed his host into the farmhouse kitchen.

CHAPTER TWENTY-SEVEN

Wolfe woke up some time short of dawn. The barn where he had bedded down on a heap of loose hay was silent. He could hear Anse MacDonald's pigs—when he introduced himself the man had chuckled about this being Old MacDonald's farm—the pigs were moving around in their pen.

They made a muted grunting sound. Wolfe did not know if that meant they were happy or sad. The feeder door clanged. Off in another direction the chickens squawked.

The sounds the pigs were making seemed normal to his untrained ears, but he had always thought the roost chickens stayed quiet until the sun came up, and that would not be for another hour or so. Not that he knew anything about chickens. Or farms. Even so...

He stood and brushed the hay stems off himself then walked over to the window at the side of the barn. Last night's moon had set and the sky was partially overcast so the darkness was probably impenetrable to anyone with normal vision. Even to Wolfe the light level was closer to dusk than daylight.

He could see well enough, though, to see the hen house door standing ajar.

Last night Aggie MacDonald had hazed all the birds inside, watered them from an old fashioned hand pump standing in the middle of the yard and carefully set the latch on the door.

Wolfe had watched the care she took with that task for the flock of chickens was one of the family's most valuable possessions. The cockerels gave them meat, and the hens gave them eggs to eat and more chicks to expand the flock.

The MacDonalds would take no chances with their chickens. Yet now the door was open? Wolfe did not think so.

He fetched his bow and slipped outside, then stopped and stood very still beside the open barn door.

There was someone in the hen house. He was fairly sure about that. He could hear the birds in there and the intruder as well. That was not so bad but he could see two other people crouched in the shadows beneath a tree by the driveway.

It was dark enough that he could not see them clearly but both held long, thin objects that he assumed were rifles or shotguns.

Not good, he thought. There were at least three people, perhaps armed with firearms, while he and MacDonald had only a bow and some primitive spear throwers to face them with.

Wolfe did not like the odds. What he needed, he decided, was to improve the balance of power.

Drifting as silent as a morning fog, Wolfe left the barn and approached the hen house door.

A dark figure was bent over a burlap sack filled with wriggling chickens. The bag was almost overflowing and probably held fifty pounds or more of the unhappy birds.

The chicken thief managed to tie the sack closed but was having trouble lifting it.

"Need a little help?" Wolfe whispered.

The thief let out a cry and stood upright.

Wolfe socked him one on the shelf of his jaw, knocking him out cold. The intruder dropped into the smelly, rather unpleasant mess on the hen house floor.

Wolfe untied the neck of the burlap sack and dumped the chickens out. The ones on the bottom were dead or dying. Smothered by the birds thrown in on top of them, he guessed, or crushed by the weight of the ones on top. MacDonald was not going to like that, but it was too late to do anything about it.

He gave a rough jerk to the unconscious thief and pulled his hands behind him then used the rope the bag had been tied with to secure the wrists together.

He pulled the cord good and tight. If the SOB suffered some that was his tough luck.

While he was doing that the fellow's cap fell off, and Wolfe discovered the intruder was no fellow at all but a woman.

He took her by the coat collar and dragged her outside where he could get a better look at her.

She was thirty or so and to put it as charitably as he knew how, not pretty. Had he wanted to be brutally honest he might have said that the poor thing was butt ugly.

She had bruises that suggested her companions were not gentle with her. Either that or she fell down an awful lot, and her hair was a stringy, greasy mess. The chicken droppings that covered the front and one side of her clothing did not add anything to her appeal.

He had her, he thought. Now what the heck was he supposed to do with her?

More to the point, what was he supposed to do with the

armed men over by the driveway who were supposed to be covering her?

Another thought occurred to him and he dashed back to the hen house, where he shooed some of the more inquisitive birds back inside and closed the door so they would not wander out into the dangers of the night.

His concern about how to handle the men with the guns was resolved when he heard a shout from behind him and the sharp report of a gunshot.

Half a heartbeat later a lead slug slammed into the hen house door a foot or so to his right.

Wolfe ducked and quickly disappeared around the back of the chicken house.

CHAPTER TWENTY-EIGHT

He heard another gunshot, but this time, had no idea what the thief was shooting at. Not him, that was for sure. A moment later, he heard a bell clanging loudly to completely shatter whatever might have been left of the predawn silence. MacDonald was obviously awake and reacting to the assault. While the scavengers' attention was on MacDonald inside the house, Wolfe slipped around behind the pig pen and approached the driveway from the side. He could see only one man in the brush there now, had no idea what had happened to the other one. One man with a gun was quite enough, however; that one raised his rifle and took aim at something in the direction of the house. Wolfe nocked an arrow on the cord and took careful aim. A broad head arrow with all the killing power of a heavy caliber rifle flashed across the driveway and struck the rifleman on the side of the head. The dark figure dropped to the ground, falling limp and unmoving.

Wolfe heard a faint crunch of gravel behind him and started to run. His head snapped forward, and he felt much more than heard the powerful blow on the back of his head.

He staggered trying to remain upright. For some reason he felt it was important for him to remain on his feet. And then, belatedly, he realized it was too late to worry about that. He was already lying face down on the ground.

Funny, he hadn't noticed himself fall. But, he must have. He could smell the heavy earth of the ground as he lay on it, and feel the chill of moisture, dew, perhaps, soaking into his shirt to reach his skin. Bits of gravel were sharp against his cheek but he did not mind that, nor the dull, deep pain that throbbed inside his head with every pulse beat of his heart.

He felt oddly detached from the pain or anxiety. He felt in fact, as if he were floating a foot or so above the ground. He rather liked the sensation. He tried to smile. The effort was interrupted when a harsh hand gripped his hair and tugged rolling him over onto his back. He could see someone kneeling over him—a woman. He found that to be strange although he did not know why. For a moment, he thought it was the woman he caught inside the henhouse, but a second look revealed she was not. This one had longer hair and a broader, flatter face. She was chunky and tough and she held a knife in her hand.

Using one hand, she lifted Wolfe's head by the hair; with the other, she laid the blade of the knife against the side of his neck. He could feel the sharp steel begin to bite and knew her intention was to slice his throat open. A rush of fear cut through the lethargy brought on by the blow to his head and he convulsed, throwing an arm up to knock her hand away.

The woman squealed in surprise and drew the knife back, but only so she could slash with it. Wolfe jerked away from her. When she followed, still trying to cut him, he grabbed hold of the wrist of her knife hand and held it tight. With his other hand, he wrapped his fingers around her throat and squeezed.

The woman shuddered and tried to pull away from him,

while at the same time trying to shove her knife into him. He held on all the tighter, squeezing all the harder. He held her like that for what seemed like a very long time. He was still squeezing when someone else bent over them and pulled the woman away while yet another person pried Wolfe's fingers away from the woman's throat.

She was choking and gasping for breath and now Wolfe was surrounded by three—no, more—five, six people, perhaps even more. Outnumbered, still groggy from the blow to the back of his head, Wolfe realized he had no chance to fight his way clear of all of them. That did not, however, mean he did not intend to try. They might well take him down, but they would not get him for free.

He would do just as much damage to them as he could before he went under.

CHAPTER TWENTY-NINE

Wolfe rolled to the side and lunged, aiming a powerful blow at the unprotected crotch of the man standing nearest him. The man doubled over in agony and Wolfe launched himself at another.

"No, Wolfe! Stop!"

MacDonald jumped in front of the man who was Wolfe's next intended target. "Stop! These people are friends!"

"Who? What?"

"Lie still. You've been hurt."

Wolfe shook his head to try to clear it. That was a serious mistake. He winced.

"You'll be alright. Just sit there. Good."

Others came to join them. One pair carried the trussed figure of the woman Wolfe caught inside the chicken coop. Two others were busy tying up the woman who had tried to cut Wolfe's throat.

He glanced into the shadows where the one he had hit with his arrow still lay.

"It's alright," MacDonald said. "She's dead."

"Your arrow..." The newcomer who had checked the

body shuddered. "It went all the way through the skull! I didn't think…" He stopped there, but his meaning was clear enough. The bow was no mere toy. It was a powerful weapon.

"'She?'" Wolfe asked.

"Yeah. All three of them were women. I've never seen a band of female scavengers before." MacDonald said.

"I guess now you can say you've seen everything."

"Sad thing is, every time I begin to believe that, something new and even more unpleasant comes along."

"Who are all these people?" Wolfe asked, looking around at the circle of badly armed men.

He saw no firearms among them. They carried an assortment of crude weapons, from MacDonald's atlatl to baseball bats, a hand sickle, knives, chains—almost anything that could inflict harm.

"They're neighbors," MacDonald explained. "We stand together. That's why I rang the bell a while ago. Attack one, and you attack us all, and we will respond to defend ourselves." He smiled. "Like a volunteer fire department, but with a slightly different purpose."

"I didn't know," Wolfe said.

MacDonald shrugged. "There wasn't any reason to think about it when we talked last night. You weren't a threat and I wasn't thinking in terms of having to defend our farm and livestock."

"That one," Wolfe motioned toward the first woman he'd seen, "killed some of your chickens."

"I saw," the farmer shrugged again. "Nothing we can do about it now, of course, but Darla and Aggie will clean and cook 'em. We'll all have a feed."

"And what about them?" Wolfe asked, inclining his head in the direction of the two captives. "What'll you do with them?"

"We'll take their weapons, of course, and whatever else they might have that we can use, but—" MacDonald's expression became grim, "they chose to attack us. They will pay the price for that."

Wolfe raised an eyebrow.

"We will hang them," MacDonald said bluntly.

"A committee of vigilance," Wolfe said softly.

"Exactly. Ours is a community of vigilance and self-defense. There's no government here, no law, so we have come together to provide our own. If you care to think about it, that is exactly how government and law came to be in the first place."

"I suppose so," Wolfe reluctantly agreed. The community of neighbors would pass judgment and mete out punishment. These two women would hang for their crimes. They would hang because they tried to steal some chickens. But, that was not really so, was it? Wolfe admitted to himself. They would hang because they attacked innocent people in the night, trying to steal what was not theirs to take, willing to kill in order to do it. After all, they were the ones with firearms. They were the first to offer the use of lethal force, there was no way to incarcerate them, and if these Idaho farmers turned the scavengers loose, they would only go elsewhere to commit more crimes, and perhaps murder other innocent folk. No, he conceded, harsh though this frontier form of justice might be, at least it was justice. He had no right to speak or act against it. On the other hand, he did not have to participate in it.

Wolfe shook his head again, not so painfully this time, and managed to crawl onto his feet. The light was beginning to grow stronger now, as dawn approached, and he pulled the welding goggles over his eyes. Thank goodness they hadn't been broken.

"Are you alright?"

"Yes, thanks."

"Go over onto the porch and Aggie will bring you breakfast and something to drink."

"No, I—thank you, but I expect I best get on the road again. I have to catch up with those people."

"What people are you looking for?" one of the neighbors asked.

"Four men traveling with a woman." Wolfe described the men as best he could, from the sketchy information he'd gotten out of Billy back at the culvert. He was able to give a much fuller description of Mrs. Crane.

"I believe I saw them!" another of the neighbors offered. "There was a group camped in the woodland south of my place...yesterday morning, it was. It could have been the people you're looking for, although I didn't approach them. I didn't bother them, and they didn't bother me or mine."

"There were four men?"

"At least three. And at least one woman. I s'pose there could have been more without me seein' 'em."

Wolfe felt a grim sort of satisfaction. He had guessed right about which road to take. The group was moving south and they were less than a day ahead of him now. Better yet, they had no idea, no way to know, he was after them.

"Mister, you helped me plenty. Thank you."

"Won't you wait until you eat?" MacDonald said.

"No... thank you, but no. I want to get moving again."

He looked at the women, who had to have heard what lay in store for them at the hands of these honest, but determined, farmers. Neither of them showed any emotion at all. Wolfe suspected they would show plenty when their time came.

"Then, give me just a moment. I want you to take that table leg that I promised you. I've already carved out the socket and drilled for the retaining board, but you'll have to find your own spears to use with it."

"You're very kind."

"Mr. Wolfe, you did my family a great favor this mornin' when you stopped these thieves. We owe you a great deal more than one ordinary table leg." MacDonald hurried away toward the house.

Wolfe excused himself from the neighbors who were clustered close around the captive women, and went to the barn to get his cart and other things. He had miles to cover.

He met old man MacDonald on the trail leaving the farm toward the main road where the old man handed over the table leg turned atlatl. Wolfe dug into his cart. "Twelve gauge?" he asked.

"For what it's worth, yeah," the farmer replied, dragging a hand over the stubble on his face.

Wolfe offered his hand. In his palm were two pristine shotgun shells.

CHAPTER THIRTY

Now that he was sure he was on the right road, Wolfe was able to concentrate on speed without having to worry about searching driveways and side roads he might pass. If he did happen to miss the scavengers—if, say, they were busy ransacking an isolated house or country store when he went by—he could satisfy himself that he was ahead of them, and simply wait for them to bring Reba to him. The more he thought about Mrs. Crane and the ordeal she was going through now, the worse he felt. Wolfe could not shake the idea that the entire thing was his fault. He should have been able to protect her, somehow. That he had not was a matter of pain, and no small amount of shame to him. He ran hard, continuing well into the night when the group ahead of him would be stopped somewhere, then finally pulled off the highway to get some rest. He expected to need his strength when he reached the gang.

He found a small creek to drink from and refill his bottles, then ate a can of beans for supper, hacking the top open with a Bowie knife, and moved well away from the stream before deciding on a place to spend what remained of the night.

He hid the cart in a thicket, and lay down beside it without bothering with a sleeping bag. The night was cool but not cold; the air moving over him felt good. The stars overhead were fiercely bright to his unshielded eyes.

Tired though he was he knew he had no need of an alarm clock to wake him come dawn. The glare of the sun would be more than harsh enough to bring him awake, even if he did oversleep.

He would, he believed, catch up with the gang of scavengers sometime the next day. He was correct about that. He saw them ahead of him late the following morning. The men moved at a strong pace, pulling Reba along at the end of a tether of some sort. Her hands were tied behind her, and the rope was looped around her neck like a leash. One of the men led Reba, while another held on to a second leash, this tied around the neck of a large dog. Wolfe assumed it was a German Shepherd, although its color made it look almost like his namesake, and while there might very well be wolves in the vicinity—perhaps escaped from the packs that were transplanted into Yellowstone National Park some years earlier—he seriously doubted that anyone would be leading one of those beasts on the end of a makeshift leash.

The other two men pushed lightly-laden grocery carts. Wolfe guessed they preferred to travel light and leave themselves plenty of room to carry home the fruits of their scavenging. Obviously, these men liked to post guards over their camps at night; otherwise MacDonald's neighbor would have seen more than just three of them stopped near his farm several nights earlier.

Wolfe tucked that bit of information away. He expected to need to know as much about these four as he possibly could; tonight, for instance. He was sure Reba would understand his delay. Better to wait until it was dark and his nocturnal vision gave him the edge. Lord knew he needed some kind of edge if he intended to take on four armed men while he had only a bow and a hatchet to oppose them.

A thrown spear would be handy in a situation like this, but so far he had not had an opportunity to make himself spears, or, just as critically important, practice with the oddly-named atlatl that MacDonald had given him. His accuracy with the bow was improving, but not as much as those vigilantes back at the farm might have thought. He had driven an arrow into the head of that scavenger. He had been aiming at her torso. Not that he was complaining; he had gotten the job done. He just hoped his luck would continue to hold.

Wolfe dropped back far enough that he would present no threat to these men, even if they did happen to spot him traveling behind them. Patiently, he trundled along the road at a swift walk and waited for the scavengers to go into camp for the night.

CHAPTER THIRTY-ONE

I t was time, he thought. The camp where the scavengers
held Reba had been silent for more than an hour. Their
fire had burned down to coals, and he hadn't seen any movement for a long time.

The thing he'd been waiting for more than anything else
was for the coals to lose their brightness. Now he could see
perfectly, while the scavengers would be blinded by the
darkness.

Wolfe began to move forward—slowly, carefully. As soon
as dark fell, he had taken up a position about a hundred
yards away from the camp. Now he needed to get closer so
that he could get a better look at them before he went in. If
he could get Reba free without a fight, he would be happy to
do it that way, but that would depend on these men and, in
particular, on the one who was posted as a guard.

He was sitting on a folding camp stool in front of a clump
of scrub oak. Very likely, he would be invisible to anyone
with normal vision, but Wolfe could see him lounging there
as clearly as if it were broad daylight.

Unfortunately, that was not entirely the advantage he had

hoped for. The man's choice of position put a tangle of dense growth at his back. Not only was the scrub oak thick, it was brittle and the ground beneath it was sure to be dry and noisy if anyone tried to move through it. The guard had picked his spot too well.

It would not be possible to approach him from behind or on either side without making a loud racket, and trying to reach him from the front would be just as difficult since he was sure to see a man-sized figure moving in the night.

Wolfe looked the guard over first then continued a careful circle around the camp. The other three men were sleeping; one of them close to the fire, the other two lying on the far side of a fallen log. The dog was tied to one of their carts. Wolfe guessed the dog was put there as a secondary guard, but did not seem much interested in the job. Wolfe could see it silently watching as he approached the camp and circled around it. He expected the dog to give a warning, but it didn't. Its ears were pricked forward, and it was alert, but it did not seem to care at all that there was a strange human there.

Reba Crane was trussed hand and foot, and had been left gagged as well. She lay close to the dying fire on the opposite side of it from the man who had chosen to sleep close to the coals. Her position looked painfully uncomfortable, and Wolfe felt twinges of renewed guilt when he saw her there. If he had only been more alert back there, he could have kept her out of this misery. Well, he would correct that now, or else.

He thought about just trying to pick her up and spirit her away, and would have done so if it hadn't been for the guard. Where Reba lay was in plain sight from the guard's post, and he would be silhouetted against the dim glow coming off the coals if he tried to reach her while the guard was watching. It would be suicidal for him to take that simple approach. Nor, unfortunately, could he try to overpower and silence the scavengers one at a time. He would have to take out the guard first, then the others one by one.

He stood for several minutes working out the sequence of movements he intended to take: first the guard, then the man farthest from the fire, then the one beside him, step over the log, and across the fire, finally, the fourth, final man. He could do it if he was lucky, if none of them woke up and shot him, if everything came together just right.

Wolfe took a deep breath and eased away from the camp and up the slight grade toward the edge of the scrub oak thicket, coming as close to the seated guard as he could manage without making noise. He pulled an arrow, one of the undamaged broad heads, off the quiver and mounted it onto the bow. Taking careful aim, he drew the arrow back until the side of his thumb was in contact with his jaw. He sighted down the arrow, aiming at the guard's head. He hated to do that, but it was the only shot that would accomplish what he needed to do; that was drop the man without him making any noise to warn the others. Certainly, it had worked well enough back at the farm, even if that shot was more accident than planned. This time, his aim was coldly deliberate. Wolfe hesitated for only a moment to offer up a prayer that he succeeded then let the missile fly.

The dog began barking furiously and lunging at the end of its leash. The night exploded into grunts and shouts and confusion.

CHAPTER THIRTY-TWO

The idiot dog wanted to go chase the flying arrow, Wolfe realized with horror. Some watchdog, now it barked. Now that it thought there was a game of fetch to be had.

The guard was as startled by the barking as Wolfe was. He turned toward the dog and that movement was enough to make Wolfe's shot miss. The arrow sailed harmlessly past the man's ear. Great.

Wolfe snatched out another arrow and hurriedly nocked it onto the string, pulling and firing before the guard, who was trying to see what had the dog upset over by the parked carts, had time to spot him. The arrow buried itself into the guard, somewhere in the upper chest. Wolfe did not know if the wound was mortal, but it certainly wiped away any interest the guard might have in anything beyond his own skin. The man dropped the pistol he had been holding in his lap and clutched at the protruding feathers with both hands before he toppled off his stool and laid writhing and kicking on the ground.

The other three were fully awake now, and waving their

guns wildly in all directions. None of them could see anything to shoot at, but one began firing anyway, blasting away into the night in the general direction of the injured guard. The bright muzzle flashes were painful to Wolfe's sensitive eyes. The man emptied his rifle magazine at nothing before one of the others snarled at him to stop wasting ammo.

While that was going on, the dog continued to bark and clamored in its eagerness to play. Wolfe felt like groaning. He could see that Reba was awake now, but tied as she was, she could not take advantage of the confusion to run away. Wolfe crouched behind the protection of a tree trunk and nocked a third arrow.

The three men beside the fire were all on their feet now, one of them cussing and hopping around on one foot while he tried to get his shoes on. The other two stood back to back, peering out into the darkness.

"Larry! Where are you, Larry? What's going on, hey?"

Wolfe assumed Larry to be the guard; Larry was not answering. Wolfe stepped out from behind the tree, pulled and fired. His arrow struck the man with one shoe off, piercing him low in the body. The scavenger doubled over, clutching himself, and dropped to the ground. He hit hard without making any effort to break his fall.

"Larry!" one of the two remaining bawled. The other, however, must have seen something. Wolfe saw the man's gun come up; he stepped hurriedly behind the tree trunk, barely in time. He heard the dull boom of the shotgun's bellow and bark and splinters filled the air on both sides of the tree.

Wolfe felt a sting on his upper arm as a stray pellet slashed across his flesh. The dog stopped barking and retreated to the far side of the cart where it was tied. The silence seemed something of a relief.

"Who are you? What's goin' on?!" one of the men shouted.

"I came for the woman!" Wolfe shouted back. "Let her go and I won't bother you again. That's all I want from you—just let her go!"

"How do we know you're tellin' the truth?"

"Mister, it won't cost you anything to find out. Just cut her loose and tell her to head for home. You won't see me again."

"We haven't seen you to begin with! Step out where we can get a look at you so's we can figure out if you're telling us the truth."

"I may be dumb, mister, but I'm not stupid."

Wolfe squatted down and peered around the tree. The two continued to stand there beside their dead fire, while the one he had hit in the belly continued to writhe. Wolfe suspected that one would soon be dead, probably the guard already was. Wolfe could no longer hear him thrashing around in the brittle oak litter.

"Let her go!" he called out again.

He loosed another arrow just over their heads. Wolfe had no idea what sort of noise it must have made coming at them, but it must have been unnerving, for they both jumped as if they had been hit instead of just startled.

"Boys, I can do that all night long. You'll never see it coming."

The men dropped low to the ground and knelt there, guns held ready, whispering back and forth. Wolfe could see them talking, but was not close enough to hear what they might be saying. After a few minutes, he called out again.

"What's it to be, fellas? Do ya want to let her go and cut your losses, or do we go to the last man standing?"

"Give us a minute, will ya?"

Wolfe could see the man straining his eyes, trying to find a target in the night so he could shoot. Wolfe crept well off to the side from where he had been and cozied up to another tree. He shot again, sending an arrow sizzling into the forearm of the man who was closer to him. The man let out a yelp and dropped his shotgun.

"Sumbitch! You done shot me!"

"Yes, and I can do it again. Now let the woman go. Next time, I aim for your head."

Again, he could plainly see as the two went into the huddle. This time, the discussion required only a few moments. The one with the injured arm stood upright, while the other one held his rifle at the ready in case Wolfe was unwary enough to show himself. The man who was on his feet took out a belt knife and bent over Reba Crane. For an awful moment, Wolfe thought he was going to get back at him by cutting her, but instead, the man slashed the ropes binding her.

Reba sat up and tore the gag out of her mouth. She spat something out and wiped her mouth with the back of her hand then said something to the men who had been her captors.

"Is that you, Jim?" she called.

"Yep, it's me. Do these men have anything of yours you want to take with you?"

"No, nothing."

"Then take off. You know which way. I'll catch up with you."

"Just a minute. There's somethin' I want to do first."

"Take your time. There's no hurry. These fellas want to shoot me, and maybe you too by now, that's all. Nothin' serious."

He could hear her laugh. That seemed a little surprising under the circumstances, but then Reba was one tough and resilient woman. She stepped carefully wide of the men beside the fire ring then ran over to the carts and reached down to untie the dog's leash. Leading the dog, Reba went out onto the road and began trotting off to the north.

"All right. I'll bid you a fond good night," Wolfe called out.

He did not, however, go anywhere. He remained where he was for the better part of an hour, watching the men to make sure they didn't try to follow Reba. They tried, with no success, to revive the one who had been struck in the belly, and went up the slope to find Larry the guard, but he was dead, too.

When they got around to building up their fire, Wolfe had to turn away from the pain of the bright flames. He ghosted away from the campsite out onto the highway and started north to retrieve his cart and catch up with Reba Crane.

He reached her just before dawn, and led her well away from the road into a thick stand of young aspen where they would be fully hidden from anyone passing by.

"We'll stop here and get rested up. Then we'll get you home, lady."

"You didn't have to do this, you know, but I'm glad you did. I don't know how to thank you enough."

Wolfe sat in the bed of fallen leaves and rubbed the dog behind his ears. It was a ferocious-looking beast, but seemed about as dangerous as a pussycat. He stopped scratching, and the dog nudged his hand, asking for more.

"You don't owe me any thanks, nor anything else. It was my fault those men had you to begin with. I'm sorry...very sorry that I let it happen."

"I'm afraid I've caused you more trouble than you know, Jim. I heard them whispering while they were deciding if they should let me go. They said they were going to come after you. You killed their buddy, Frank, and they want revenge. They intend to hunt you down and kill you if it takes them all year long."

The dog whined and scratched at Wolfe's arm until he began to rub its ears again.

"We'll worry about that if and when they try it," he smiled. "In the meantime, ma'am, let's be gettin' you back to your family."

And then, he thought, maybe—please, God—just maybe he could take himself back to his family, too.

THE END

ABOUT THE AUTHOR

Frank Roderus has been writing full time for more than thirty years and "still loves every minute of the doing," he says. "I am truly blessed to be able to make a living doing what I love so very much to do. I wrote my first story—it was a western—when I was five. It was really awful, as might be expected, but my mother kept that typed and spell-checked (my mother again) short story tucked away until the day she died. Later I became a newspaper reporter, thinking that books are written by authors which I most assuredly was not. I kept trying to write, though, eventually did it wrong enough to learn how to get it right. That first sale, a young adult novel published by Independence Press, was more than thirty years and a good many books ago and I have loved every day since. Did I mention how very blessed I am? Believe it."

Frank passed away in 2015, but his stories live on. The Night-walker series never saw the light of day while Frank lived, but the books are available now. Enjoy the story.

NOTES - CRAIG MARTELLE

I never met Frank while he lived, but he is the kind of guy I would have enjoyed hanging out with, sipping a cold beer and talking. He was from an older generation (I'm fifty-six when writing this, but he reminds me of my grandfather, even though my dad is now eighty-two years old). Frank strikes me as a gentleman, an honorable soul who wasn't afraid of hard work.

These stories were discovered after Frank passed and were picked up by Wolfpack Publishing, but that is a group dedicated to westerns. This is a post-apocalyptic series. I am blessed, like Frank, in that I have met some incredible people in this industry. My forte is post-apoc, so it seemed a nice fit to take over these stories and finish them. Frank had written three and a half short books. I was able to finish the fourth book, which doesn't complete the story arc. There are plenty of James Wolfe's adventures remaining. I hope you, good reader, enjoy this tale, spun about a different time, written in Frank's conversational tone.

There are lessons in here that we can all take to heart. I say sir and ma'am, say please and thank you. As an author, I understand that our words matter. As a human, I know that my actions are even more important. Combine the two and you have the bedrock of a civilized society. It starts with us. I can only control me, so that's what I do. I hope my story crafting and Frank's show you that people like us still exist.

I live 150 miles from the Arctic Circle in the Alaskan interior, a little town called Fox on the outskirts of the sprawling city known as Fairbanks with all 30,000 of its residents. It's as big city as I like. Can you see why post-apocalyptic survival is on my mind? We always plan to be without power for thirty days. We store six months' worth of water, groceries, and dog food. I have electricity as a utility. Everything else has to be trucked in or out. A water tank. A fuel oil tank. Dual propane tanks. A septic tank. And a pellet stove. I know. I should have a woodburner for true survival as you can't cook on a pellet stove and you can't buy pellets, but I do like my conveniences. Take coffee for example.

I like my coffee. I usually keep a years' supply on hand. Old coffee is better than no coffee.

We can watch the northern lights from our driveway. We live away from any light pollution. The last days of March, 2019 have been spectacular, vivid and active shows in the clear sky. It's still dark enough to see the aurora, but soon it won't be. We have twenty-fours of daylight for a couple months around the summer solstice. In the winter, we aren't dark that long, but on December 21st, we have less than four hours where the sun is above the southern horizon.

The sun rises in the south and sets in the south during the winter. In the summer, the sun doesn't set. The compass points in an odd direction, definitely not toward the North Pole, but toward Siberia because of the magnetic shift that's going on. The town of North Pole, Alaska is thirty miles to the south. An oddity to be sure, but just how it is where I live.

There's a lot to be said living this far away from humanity. We have a great deal of peace, unless a visiting moose wreaks havoc on our garden. Or the UPS driver sends our dog into a frenzy. Everything we need is right here.

That's enough about me – look for Nightwalker 2, 3, and 4 coming soon. They are all ready, just need to spin out of the queue and into your Kindle. We'll see what kind of feedback we get before we continue the series. James Wolfe has a long ways to go and time is not on his side.

BOOKS BY CRAIG MARTELLE

Craig Martelle's other books (listed by series)

Terry Henry Walton Chronicles (co-written with Michael Anderle) – a post-apocalyptic paranormal adventure

Gateway to the Universe (co-written with Justin Sloan & Michael Anderle) – this book transitions the characters from the Terry Henry Walton Chronicles to The Bad Company

The Bad Company (co-written with Michael Anderle) – a military science fiction space opera

End Times Alaska (also available in audio) – a Permuted Press publication – a post-apocalyptic survivalist adventure

The Free Trader – a Young Adult Science Fiction Action Adventure

Cygnus Space Opera – A Young Adult Space Opera (set in the Free Trader universe)

Darklanding (co-written with Scott Moon) – a Space Western

Rick Banik – Spy & Terrorism Action Adventure

Become a Successful Indie Author – a non-fiction work

Enemy of my Enemy (co-written with Tim Marquitz) – a galactic alien military space opera

Superdreadnought (co-written with Tim Marquitz) – a military space opera

Metal Legion (co-written with Caleb Wachter) - a military space opera

End Days (co-written with E.E. Isherwood) – a post-apocalyptic adventure

Mystically Engineered (co-written with Valerie Emerson) – dragons in space

Monster Case Files (co-written with Kathryn Hearst) – a young-adult cozy mystery series

For a complete list of books from Craig, please see www.craigmartelle.com